THE WINKING RUBY MYSTERY

"Save Carlo . . . winking ruby . . . hurry!" This plea uttered by a young violinist, just before he lapsed into a coma, launch Louise and Jean Dana on an exciting trip to Europe.

Danger stalks the teen-age detectives from the moment they board the *Balaska* with their Uncle Ned, captain of the ocean liner. Crossing the Atlantic they meet Enrico and Lena Dotti, professional hypnotists, who offer to help in solving the puzzle but turn out to be dangerous enemies.

In Europe, while probing deeper into the strange riddle, Louise and Jean become enmeshed in a mystery more frightening than the dungeon in which they find themselves imprisoned. How they escape and locate a fabulous crimson gem will thrill all Carolyn Keene fans.

"You've stolen my priceless ruby ring!"
Mrs. Cracken cried.

The *Dana Girls* Mystery Stories

THE
WINKING RUBY
MYSTERY

By Carolyn Keene

GROSSET & DUNLAP
Publishers   New York

PRINTED IN THE UNITED STATES OF AMERICA

CONTENTS

CHAPTER I

A Shipboard Mystery

"How would you girls like to solve a mystery while you're in Europe?"

The speaker was the Dana girls' uncle, captain of the ocean liner *Balaska*.

"Uncle Ned, you mean—" Louise, an attractive brunette of seventeen, was too excited to finish the sentence.

Her sister Jean, sixteen, gave the sturdy, ruddy-faced captain a hug. "We're really going on your next trip? You managed to get reservations?" the pretty, blond-haired girl asked.

"That I did, my hearties," Captain Dana replied. "Just received word about last-minute cancellations. And there's a cabin for your Aunt Harriet too."

Across the comfortably furnished living room, where the family had gathered, sat the petite, middle-aged sister of Uncle Ned. These two relatives had acted as mother and father to Louise and Jean since the death of the girls' parents many years before.

Louise gazed at her uncle affectionately. "That's wonderful—simply wonderful! And now, tell us what the mystery is."

"Well," Captain Dana began, "something most mysterious happened on board the *Balaska* just before we docked in New York. In our ship's orchestra was a violinist named Gino Marzi. He's an Italian, about twenty-five, and an excellent musician. He's made several records.

"I received a sudden call our last morning out that he was very ill and wanted to see me at once. When I arrived in his stateroom, he grabbed my hand and gasped, 'Please, Captain, save Carlo . . . winking ruby . . . hurry!' That was all."

"How strange!" murmured Aunt Harriet. "Is Mr. Marzi still living?"

"Yes," her brother answered. "But directly after he gave me the message, he lapsed into a coma. Right now, Gino is in a New York hospital. He regained consciousness but is suffering from amnesia. The poor man can't even remember how to play the violin."

"How tragic," said Jean. Usually vivacious, her blue eyes were now full of sympathy. "So he can't remember who he is and can't tell you about his family?"

"Oh, I know that he has a mother and a sister

with whom he lives in Italy," Uncle Ned told his niece. "I sent word to them at the address he had given when taking the job, but the cable wasn't delivered. His relatives couldn't be found."

Louise leaned forward in her chair. "Is finding them part of the mystery Jean and I are to solve?" When Captain Dana nodded, she asked, "How about the person Gino mentioned named Carlo? Who is he?"

"I don't know, nor did anyone else on the ship," Uncle Ned replied. "And the message about the winking ruby is a complete enigma."

Aunt Harriet asked her brother why Gino Marzi had turned to him for help.

The captain smiled broadly. "I guess I've boasted a bit from time to time about my nieces' sleuthing ability. I had told Gino you girls would soon be home from your Western trip and I hoped to take you abroad."

"Clue number one," said Jean. "You think Carlo is probably in Europe?"

"Yes," Captain Dana replied. "No doubt he's in Italy, and may be in Firenze where the Marzis used to live."

"Firenze? You mean the city we Americans call Florence?" Louise asked.

"Yes. But in Italian it is called Firenze."

"Then Firenze it is," stated Jean with a laugh. "And are we going there?"

"I have plane reservations for you three from

London to Firenze," Uncle Ned said. "We'll dock at Southampton in England and go by car to London." Suddenly he glanced at his wrist watch, then jumped up. "I nearly forgot! Our plane leaves from the Oak Falls airport in two hours. Better get your gear stowed in a hurry!"

The girls and their aunt fairly flew out of their chairs and across the room. Louise and Jean bounded up the stairway, while Aunt Harriet rushed to the kitchen to speak to Cora Appel, the maid.

Cora was a rather scatterbrained young woman, and Miss Dana felt she could not depend on her to close the house properly. Whenever Cora had to hurry she became flustered and clumsy. Now, as Aunt Harriet told her of the sudden plan to go to Europe and that she was to pack at once and pay her family a visit while they were gone, Cora stared in stupefaction.

"I can't do it. My things've got to be washed and ironed first," she objected.

"You'll have to take them as they are," Miss Dana told her hurriedly. "Please go to the attic and bring down your bag and my large green suitcase, Cora. The captain will drive you to the railroad station. There's a train to your home town every hour. I'll give you vacation money."

As if in a daze, Cora hung her apron in the closet and started up the stairway. At the girls' room she paused to tell them of her errand, then continued to the third floor. The sisters could hear her moving pieces of furniture and trunks.

"The luggage is in plain sight and Applecore can't see it," Jean said, using a nickname the sisters had given the girl. Finally Jean went to the foot of the attic stairs and called out, "Cora! Please hurry!"

"I'm a-comin'," Cora answered.

The next moment she appeared at the top of the steps with a bag in each hand. Cora extended one foot toward the step below, but missed it completely. She swayed a moment, trying to recover her balance, then pitched forward.

There was a blur of flying suitcases and a cry of fright as Cora tumbled down the stairs. A moment later she and the bags landed in the hall below. Jean grabbed the maid in time to keep her head from striking the floor.

"Oh, I'm terribly sorry," Jean said kindly. "Are you hurt?"

"I guess not—much. But look at Miss Dana's bag. The lock broke clean off!"

The commotion brought the other Danas to the scene. Assured by Cora that she was uninjured, Captain Dana looked at the broken lock.

"Hm!" he said. "I'll have to find a new lock for this. I'll take the bag downtown and have one put on."

Less than five minutes after he left the house, Louise was startled by a scream of pain from Cora.

Rushing into her room at the end of the long second-floor hall, Louise heard the maid babbling:

"It's numb! I can't move it. My arm must be
broken. Somebody help me!"

"Cora, what happened?"

The maid pointed to her right arm, which she
could not raise, and wailed that there was no feeling in it.

Louise was worried. "I'll call a doctor right
away, Cora. Lie down until he comes."

Though Louise phoned several physicians, none
was available at the moment. "I'll have to take
Cora to the hospital," she told Jean and Aunt Harriet. "I wish Uncle Ned would come back with
the car."

"Why not ask Mrs. Drake if we may borrow
hers?" Aunt Harriet suggested.

Louise hastened next door to their neighbor.
Mrs. Drake generously offered the use of her sedan.
As Louise backed the car out of the garage, Jean
helped Cora walk to the driveway.

At the hospital Louise and Cora found several
patients ahead of them in the emergency clinic.
As the maid sat weeping, Louise tried to comfort
her. She also looked at her watch worriedly every
two minutes. There was a chance she would miss
the plane to New York.

Finally a nurse came up to them and led Cora
and Louise into a doctor's office. After an examination of the injured arm, he said, "It feels numb,

young lady, because you've sustained a slight shoulder separation. Your arm will be all right in a few days."

"It's not broken?" Cora asked him.

The doctor laughed. "Of course not." He looked at her patiently. "You seem disappointed. Cheer up!" Cora forced a smile.

The doctor pulled the separation together and bound the arm with adhesive tape.

When the girls returned to the Dana house, Aunt Harriet and Jean packed the maid's bag. Uncle Ned, who had just returned with the repaired suitcase, said he would drive Cora to the train.

"Good-by!" the girl called out from the car. "Have a good time, folks, and send me some picture cards."

By the time Uncle Ned returned from the station, the travelers' bags were completely packed and a taxi ordered. Captain Dana locked the house and garage carefully. Then he notified the police that the premises would be vacant for a while.

"Now I guess we're ready to set sail," the captain announced as the taxi drove up. Everyone got in quickly, for there was not a moment to lose.

"My, you all look so pretty," Uncle Ned said admiringly, surveying his family as the taxi started off.

Jean wore a royal-blue summer suit, attractively accented by a lighter blue scarf at the neck. Her sister's brunette beauty and lovely coloring were heightened by a rose-colored suit and a pale-pink sleeveless blouse. Aunt Harriet looked smart in a beige dress with a matching lightweight coat.

The Danas reached the airport just in time to make their plane and they hurriedly scrambled aboard. The only two double seats still vacant were far forward and at the very rear.

Jean and her uncle sat together, right behind the pilot's compartment, while Louise and Aunt Harriet took the rear seats. After the plane was high in the air and the Oak Falls airport had receded from view, Jean turned to Captain Dana and asked him to tell her more about Gino Marzi.

"He's a very fine young fellow," Uncle Ned replied. "But the poor man always had a sad expression. He seemed to be worried about something."

"He never told you what bothered him?" Jean queried.

"No. Gino was a quiet fellow. He was well liked on board ship, but he never made close friends."

Jean asked her uncle if he had any idea as to what the winking ruby might be. When he shook his head, Jean said she had. "It could be a gem, a secret code word, or," his niece added with a laugh, "a flirtatious girl!"

Uncle Ned smiled. "Whatever it is, I have every

confidence that you and Louise will find out before this trip is over."

"A big order, Uncle Ned," said Jean with a mock sigh. Then she sobered. "Uncle Ned, do you think that if we can find Carlo and save his life, Gino's memory will be restored?"

"I haven't a doubt of it," Captain Dana replied. "In fact, the doctor said that very thing."

Jean became thoughtful. This was indeed a challenge to her and Louise. One person's life perhaps at stake and another's in a dazed, confused state!

The nonstop flight to New York was smooth, and before the Danas realized they had covered so many miles, the big plane was landing at the municipal airport. They took a taxi directly to the *Balaska*, and after showing their passports, went aboard.

"Oh, I just can't believe it!" said Louise. "To think we're going to Europe again!"

"And with an exciting mystery to solve," Jean added.

Many passengers and visitors were milling about and in the distance the ship's orchestra could be heard. There was an excited, festive air on the *Balaska*.

Captain Dana led his family to the main lobby and introduced them to the purser, Mr. Wingate. He was a tall, pleasant man, but had a stern air of authority as he stood behind the counter of his office.

"I'm very glad we had some cancellations," Mr. Wingate said. "Your stateroom, Miss Dana, is 324 and the girls have 326 next to it."

Uncle Ned had to leave his family now, so Aunt Harriet and the girls went off to find their rooms. As Jean and Louise walked into 326, smiles broke out on their faces. On the bureau was a large bouquet, a fresh fruit arrangement, and an intriguing-looking covered wicker basket.

"Oh, I wonder who sent this," said Louise, hurrying over to the basket.

She looked at the card attached to it and frowned in amazement.

"Carlo!" she cried out. "How strange!"

Louise flipped open the cover of the basket. The next instant she jumped back, giving a scream.

CHAPTER II

The Snake Chase

As LOUISE pulled back in panic, a snake reared its head from the basket. The reptile's forked tongue darted out and its fangs would have struck Louise if she had not moved so quickly.

"A poisonous copperhead!" Jean cried out.

The snake rose higher and was about to slither over the edge of the basket when Jean leaped forward. She whipped off her shoe and hit the reptile on the head. It recoiled and Jean slammed down the lid of the basket, and fastened the clasp.

"Oh!" Louise sank down onto her bed. "If that snake had bitten me— Thanks, Jean."

"What a terrible trick!" her sister declared furiously.

She glared at the basket, then picked up the card attached to it. It was plain white and tied to the handle with a cord.

"Well," she remarked, "we're involved in this mystery for sure, Louise."

"Yes, Jean, do you suppose the Carlo who sent this is the one that Gino Marzi referred to?"

Jean frowned. "That would mean he's in America," she said. "But Uncle Ned was sure he must be in Italy."

"Then this means," said Louise, "that the man who sent the snake was using his name."

"Exactly. But why?"

"I think someone is trying to frighten us and keep us from solving the mystery," Louise replied.

Had he known the Dana girls, the mysterious stranger would have realized that this was futile. In their first adventure, *Mystery of the Stone Tiger*, Louise and Jean had tracked down a ghost terrifying the people in their home town. Recently out West they had solved the puzzle of *The Secret of Lost Lake* as they searched for a witch reputedly haunting the site of an isolated community buried by a landslide years ago.

Now Jean smiled at Louise and said, "We'll probably run into more danger while we're on this case. But I'm ready for it!"

"Yes," Louise agreed. "The first thing we'd better do is get rid of the snake, and then try to find out who delivered it."

She pressed a wall button to summon the room steward. While waiting for him to arrive, the girls took off their suit jackets and hung them up. Each girl wore an attractive colored blouse.

In a few minutes a small blond man, about fifty

years old, came to their door. He was dressed in dark trousers and a white coat.

"Yes? Can I be of service to you?" he asked pleasantly. "I'm Archie, your room steward."

The smile he wore quickly faded when Louise told him what the basket contained. Archie said he knew nothing about it. He had not been around when the basket was delivered.

"Then who brought the snake to our cabin?" Jean asked.

"Suppose we ask Mr. Wingate," Archie suggested. He picked up the telephone and called the purser's office. But neither Mr. Wingate nor his assistant knew anything about the basket.

"I suppose any one of a number of people might have brought the snake aboard," Jean said, sighing.

"Yes," Archie replied. "It could have been a passenger, a visitor, an officer, or a member of the crew. It will be pretty hard to find out right now. We're very busy just before sailing time, you know."

The steward suggested that the girls get in touch with Captain Dana at once. It was a serious matter and the captain should be told of the incident. Louise phoned her uncle, who came immediately to the stateroom.

The hubbub also brought Aunt Harriet. She, too, was alarmed over the turn of events.

"This is dreadful!" she exclaimed. "Maybe you girls had better make it known that you're not

going to have anything to do with carrying out
Mr. Marzi's request."

"Oh, Aunty, please!" her nieces chorused.

"Well, if your uncle thinks it's all right to continue sleuthing I won't stop you," Aunt Harriet
agreed reluctantly.

"Of course they'll continue," said her brother.
"Nothing's going to scare a Dana from a mystery!"

But Captain Dana's face was red with anger.
He declared that he himself would try to find out
who had brought the snake aboard.

"In the meantime, I'll get hold of a taximan to
take this thing up to the zoo."

He stormed out of the room and within ten
minutes a cab driver appeared at the door. He
looked uneasily at the basket, and particularly at
the clasp, which was not a very secure one. He
agreed, however, to take the snake away.

"I'll be glad, though, when this fellow is up at
the zoo," he paid, picking up the handle gingerly.

As the driver reached the doorway, he almost
collided with a passenger in the corridor. In back-
ing out of the way, the taximan caught the handle
of the basket on the doorknob. The lid ripped
open and, to everyone's horror, the snake slithered
onto the floor.

"Oh, good night!" the driver cried out, and a
couple of women passing by shrieked in fright.

Louise grabbed the basket and went after the
snake, which was wriggling with lightning speed

The snake slithered onto the floor.

down the corridor. As it reached Aunt Harriet's stateroom, the reptile turned in.

Suddenly a voice behind Louise said, "I'll fix him! Just let me get at him!"

The girl turned to see the steward, Archie, with a spray gun in his hands. It was the kind used to kill flies and mosquitoes.

Archie dashed into the room and pumped the spray vigorously at the snake's head. In a few seconds the liquid had the desired effect. The snake, overcome with the fumes, stopped wriggling and lay still.

Louise held the basket as Archie picked up the reptile and dropped it inside. The lid was closed and the basket once more locked. To be sure the snake could not get out again, Archie procured some cord and tied it around the clasp.

"What a fright!" said Aunt Harriet after the man had left with the basket.

She suggested that possibly other sinister things were hidden in the girls' room. Quickly the three searched every inch of it, then Miss Dana's room as well. They found nothing unusual.

"But something else may happen," Aunt Harriet prophesied with a sigh.

Louise put an arm around her. "Please stop worrying," she begged. "Jean and I will be very careful. We promise."

Miss Dana smiled. "All right, dear. But I can't help worrying when I think of some of the predicaments you two have gotten into while solving mysteries."

At this moment Archie came to the door. He told them he had been thinking about the snake and its mysterious sender.

"You know who might help you?" the steward said. "There's a couple on board who are hypnotists, Enrico and Lena Dotti. They came over with us from Europe and they're going back. The Dottis can really put people to sleep and make them talk. If you see somebody you're suspicious about, the Dottis might be able to find out if he brought the snake aboard."

"Thank you very much for your suggestion," Louise said. "Maybe we'll do that."

The Danas doubted that this would be a very practical method for unmasking the culprit. But they were interested to hear about the hypnotists and curious to see them at work.

Jean and Louise smiled at the steward. "Of course, if it were a visitor who brought the snake aboard, the hypnotists couldn't help us."

Archie admitted that this was true, but said he was just trying to be helpful. When the steward left, Jean said:

"Louise, we haven't looked at the cards on our presents to see who sent them!"

Both girls laughed at the oversight and began to open the small envelopes attached to the gifts. The pretty bouquet was from the steamship line, with a note saying that the company was delighted to have Captain Dana's sister and nieces making the trip.

The fruit arrangement was from two boys who dated the Dana girls quite often. They were Ken Scott, who was Louise's escort, and Chris Barton, Jean's friend. Both boys attended Walton Academy near Starhurst.

"What a beautiful apple!" Louise exclaimed. "But how in the world did the boys learn we're sailing? We didn't know it ourselves until a few hours ago."

"Oh, I forgot!" said Jean. "While you were at the hospital with Applecore, the boys phoned from New York and I told them about our trip. They would have come to see us off, but were leaving shortly by train for the West."

Louise, who was facing the door, smiled, then her expression changed to one of complete wonder. Jean turned to see what had suddenly caught her sister's attention.

She, too, gasped in surprise at two girls who stood in the doorway!

CHAPTER III

Strange Signals

"EVELYN! Doris!" the Dana girls cried out, dashing across the stateroom to greet their two best friends from Starhurst School.

"Surprised?" asked Evelyn Starr, a tall, slender, dark-haired girl. Ordinarily shy, Evelyn was so loyal to the Danas that she never hesitated to brave danger to help them.

"Are we surprised!" Louise exclaimed. "This makes our sailing perfect! But how in the world did you ever find out we were really going?"

Blond, pretty Doris Harland looked at Evelyn and said, "Shall we tell them?"

"Yes," agreed Evelyn, her eyes twinkling.

Giggling, the two newcomers announced that they were accompanying the Danas to Europe.

"We've kept it a secret for weeks," Doris went on. "Your uncle and aunt asked my folks and Evelyn's brother to let us go if the *Balaska* had accommodations. What a race we had after your uncle telephoned the good news this morning!"

Jean put her hands on her friends' shoulders. "Do you mean this? Are you really going with us?"

"We'll prove it," said Evelyn gaily, and led the way to a stateroom on the far side of Aunt Harriet's. "This is ours all the way to Southampton," she said.

"You know," said Doris, chuckling, "it's a good thing Evelyn and I got passports this spring, because you can't get them nowadays on five minutes' notice."

Just then the *Balaska's* horn gave a loud, raucous whistle. As the sound died away, a steward in the corridor cried out, "All ashore that's going ashore!"

"Let's hurry out on deck," Jean suggested.

The Danas told Aunt Harriet their plans, then locked the cabin door. As an extra precaution against further unwanted deliveries, they asked Archie to watch 326 until after the ship had left the dock.

On deck there was confusion, laughter, and farewell songs. Visitors hugged their friends, wished them *bon voyage*, then pushed along with the crowd toward the gangplank.

A thrill of anticipation filled the girls. They edged their way through the gay, struggling throng of people until they found places at the rail.

"Look at that crowd on the dock!" exclaimed Doris. "It's enormous!"

People were waving and throwing colored paper streamers toward the ship's deck. Passengers near the railing were tossing some to the dock, so that soon there was a crisscrossed mass of the ribbon.

Some of it had curled around the girls' heads and Doris said laughingly, "Isn't this thrilling!"

Louise giggled. "I feel as if I'm at a New Year's Eve party!"

There were more blasts of the horn, mingled with music by the ship's band. In the din it was impossible for anyone on deck to hear what friends ashore were trying to call out to them.

Several tried giving messages in sign language and the Danas were amused by the gestures. Presently the sisters' attention was caught by a red-haired man below them who was neither smiling nor acting as if he were in a happy mood. He scowled at the people waving their arms in front of him and cutting off his vision as he tried to signal someone on board.

"Look!" Louise suddenly whispered to Jean. "Did you see what I saw?"

"Yes. That man was forming the letter L and the letter J with his fingers!" replied her sister.

"Do you think he was referring to us?" Louise asked.

Jean did not reply as she stared down intently at the man. Now she could see him wink first one eye, then the other. A moment later he pointed to the little finger of his left hand at the spot where a ring might be worn. He had none on.

"I wish I could see whom he's signaling to," Jean said, as she leaned over the railing and looked to her right. "Too many people are in the way. I'll walk in that direction and try to find the person."

Jean hurried toward the area where she assumed the passenger might be, while Louise continued to watch the man on the pier.

In a few minutes the gangplank was removed. There were more blasts of the horn, then slowly the ocean liner began to move away from the dock.

At this moment the red-haired man was forming the letter V on his fingers. Then he clasped his hands together, as if in a handshake of good luck to his friend on board the *Balaska*.

"See that red-haired man down there?" said Louise to her two friends. "I have a hunch he has something to do with our mystery of Carlo and the winking ruby."

Evelyn and Doris looked at him. Then, amazed, they turned to Louise. "You mean," said Doris, "that you've already started working on a mystery?"

"Yes. I'll tell you about it later," said Louise.

She continued to watch the red-haired man until the ship was out in midstream and she could no longer distinguish him from the rest of the crowd.

In the meantime, the passengers along the rail began to disperse. Jean looked at each one intently but it was impossible for her to determine the person to whom the red-haired man might have been signaling. Finally she joined her sister and the other girls, reporting failure.

"But one thing I'm convinced of," she said, "is that someone connected with our mystery is a passenger on this ship."

In whispers the Danas told their friends about Gino Marzi and his mysterious request to Uncle Ned.

"Gino Marzi?" Doris repeated. "Why, just the other day I heard a record of his. It was marvelous. You mean he may never play again?"

"Not unless his memory is restored," Louise answered worriedly. "But we hope to help do that."

"Well, I certainly want to help in solving the mystery," Doris declared. "He's a wonderful musician."

"Count me in," said Evelyn. "But don't make this mystery too dangerous."

"We can't promise that," Jean replied, then told their friends of the snake episode.

"Ugh!" said Doris. "I'm glad I wasn't here."

Evelyn sighed. "I can see plenty of adventure ahead. But right now let's enjoy the beginning of our trip."

For the next half hour the girls watched the skyscraper skyline of New York recede, and waved to the Statue of Liberty as the ship moved down the bay. When they were far out of the harbor, however, the Danas' minds returned once more to the mystery they hoped to solve.

"Let's walk around," Jean suggested, "and see if we can find any passenger wearing a ruby ring. Perhaps the man on the dock was signaling to a person wearing one."

The four girls walked the length of the ship on each deck, glancing casually at passengers' fingers. They did not see one ruby ring.

"Let's try something else," Louise proposed. "We'll ask the ship's officers about Gino Marzi."

The girls divided this investigation work, with Evelyn accompanying Louise and Doris trailing Jean. When they met in the Danas' stateroom an hour later to exchange information, all of them had learned exactly the same thing: none of the officers or the ship's doctor knew any more about Gino Marzi than Captain Dana did. He was considered by all of them to be a fine young man, and they felt great sympathy for him now.

"Well, what's the next move?" asked Evelyn.

Louise told her of Archie's mention of the hypnotists on board. "They may know something about Gino Marzi. Let's call on them."

The four girls went to the Dottis' suite, which consisted of two rooms. The hypnotists used the inner one for their treatments. A sign on the wall announced:

HEALTH IMPROVEMENT THROUGH HYPNOTISM

The Dottis greeted their callers cordially and invited them into the inner room. Enrico, an Italian-American, about forty-five, was dark, slender, and wore a small mustache. His wife Lena, a petite blond, smiled continually in a somewhat forced manner.

"Did you come for a hypnotic treatment?" she asked.

"Not now," Louise replied pleasantly. "We'd just like to ask you a few questions. Jean and I are Captain Dana's nieces. He told us what happened to the violinist Gino Marzi on the trip over. We wondered if you might have learned anything from him which might help us locate some of his relatives."

The smile faded from Lena Dotti's face. "That Gino Marzi!" she said, sniffing as if annoyed. "We can't help you find his relatives. But one thing we do know. I don't want to seem harsh, but Gino's mentally unsound. The true story is that he was jilted by his girl and has never been the same since."

"That's right," Enrico spoke up. "We urged Gino to let us give him treatments. We might have cured him but he refused."

So the violinist had confided in the hypnotists! Suddenly Louise had an idea. "Mr. and Mrs. Dotti," she said, "perhaps you can tell us about a certain friend of Gino's. His name is Carlo!"

CHAPTER IV

A Lost Gem

Enrico and Lena Dotti exchanged glances. The
Danas thought that they detected an almost im-
perceptible look of fright and a warning to each
other not to say anything. Why? Did they feel they
had said too much already?

"We know of no one by the name of Carlo,"
Enrico answered. Then, looking hard at Louise,
he said, "What makes you ask?"

Louise decided not to tell him. But Doris, thinking she might help solve this part of the mystery,
impulsively revealed to the couple the entire story
of the snake.

"It was a dreadful thing to do, and scared
Louise and Jean half out of their wits," she went
on. "I think if you know who this Carlo is, you
ought to tell us."

At this remark Lena bristled. "We told you we
don't know anyone named Carlo and we don't!"

"That's right," Enrico echoed.

Embarrassed, Doris said no more. The girls were about to turn and leave when Enrico said quickly, "Don't be in a hurry. I have a theory about that snake."

The girls paused and waited for him to go on, as his wife stepped into the outer room.

"Girls as pretty as you are must have lots of admirers," the hypnotist said, smiling. "I'm sure the snake was harmless and some boy friend of yours sent it for a joke."

Doris and Evelyn were startled to hear this. Could Ken and Chris have sent the reptile with the flowers just to tease the Danas?

"The snake wasn't harmless," Jean retorted, "and our friends wouldn't play a dangerous trick like that!"

Just then, Lena Dotti called from the doorway, "Enrico, our next patient is here for a treatment."

At once the man put on a flowing red-and-gold robe which lay on a couch. Then he picked up a turban of the same material and placed it on his head.

"Please come to see us again some time," he invited his four callers. "Surely you must have problems and under a hypnotic state you could easily have them solved."

The girls thanked him and his wife, saying they would think about it.

On the way to their staterooms, Jean shuddered.

"Maybe that man is a good hypnotist, but I wouldn't want him to put me under a spell! Somehow I just don't like him!"

"Or his wife," Doris put in.

The others agreed, and Evelyn remarked, "Another blind alley. I suppose the next thing to do is interview the crew to find out if anyone knows Carlo or who sent the snake."

"Yes," Louise agreed, but added that now would probably not be a good time. The staff were busy helping the passengers get settled, while those connected with the dining room and kitchens would be making dinner preparations.

"Oh, that reminds me," said Doris. "I read on the bulletin board that they'll be serving tea soon. Let's go on deck and have some."

The Danas stopped at Aunt Harriet's stateroom to take her along but found she had already left. Archie told them that she had gone on deck to rent chairs for the trip. The girls hurried outside and located Miss Dana near the entrance to one of the lounges. She had already reserved five chairs in the sheltered spot.

"I'm glad you've joined me," Aunt Harriet said. "I was beginning to wonder if you were so busy with the mystery that you weren't going to have tea with me."

Soon the deck steward came along, rolling a cart before him. When he reached the Dana group the man stopped and offered them not only tea but sandwiches and *petits fours*. While the group lounged in the reclining deck chairs, drinking tea and munching the delicious little sandwiches, the girls told their aunt of having failed so far to turn up a single clue.

"That's too bad," said Aunt Harriet. "But the trip has only begun. You have several days in which to work."

The words were hardly spoken, when Jean, who was looking down the deck, moved so quickly that she spilled some of her tea.

"What do you see?" Louise asked her.

"A ruby ring!" her sister answered in a low voice.

Everyone in the group turned to look at a large, flashily dressed, middle-aged woman who was coming in their direction. On the little finger of her left hand was a ring which contained a very large beautiful gem! When she reached the entrance to the lounge, the woman turned and swept inside.

"Let's follow her, Louise," urged Jean.

The two sisters hastily deposited their teacups on the deck and hurried after the stranger. Jean suggested rushing up and speaking to her, but Louise held her sister back. "First, let's try to find out who she is."

Jean agreed and they walked at a discreet distance behind her. A few minutes later the woman paused before the door of stateroom 415, took a key from her purse, and entered.

"Now we can find out from the purser who she is," said Louise.

The Danas went to Mr. Wingate's office and asked him who was occupying 415. He looked up his list of passengers, then replied:

"Miss Rosamunde la Mer has that suite."

"Rosamunde la Mer!" Louise exclaimed. "The famous night-club singer?"

Mr. Wingate nodded. "She's the one."

"Thank you," said Louise, and the girls walked back toward their deck chairs.

"Louise," said Jean, "do you think that red-haired man on the dock might have been referring to her ring? And that it might even be the winking ruby?"

Louise thought this was highly possible. "Maybe he has a partner on board the *Balaska* who intends to steal the ring!" she suggested.

"Do you think we should warn Miss la Mer?" Jean asked.

"I don't know," Louise answered. "Let's ask Aunt Harriet's advice."

When Louise asked Miss Dana for her opinion, Aunt Harriet thought for a moment, then replied, "I believe you girls are making a mountain out of a molehill. I'm afraid that Miss la Mer would feel you were being presumptuous if you made such a suggestion to her. Let's wait until dinnertime and ask your uncle what to do."

Doris suddenly laughed. "We've hardly left New York and already everything's complicated!"

Evelyn grinned too. "Doris," she said, "don't *you* know that's what Louise and Jean thrive on?"

Miss la Mer was forgotten for the moment. The girls spent the balance of the afternoon investigating the various recreational activities which the *Balaska* offered. They decided to enter a ping-pong tournament which was posted and to take advantage of the swimming pool during the trip.

"This ship is just heavenly!" Doris remarked, as the girls went to their staterooms to dress for dinner. "Your uncle certainly is a dear to have made it possible for us to come."

"We're pretty thrilled ourselves," said Louise.

She and Jean were ready long before the others. Louise had put on a dressy cotton, and Jean a light-blue linen skirt and beaded sweater. They told their aunt and friends that they would meet them on deck.

"We want to see the end of the beautiful sunset and watch the moon rise," said Louise.

As the sisters stepped from the lounge door onto the deck, Jean grasped Louise's arm. "Look! There's Enrico Dotti talking to Rosamunde la Mer!"

Louise glanced in the couple's direction. They were leaning against the rail, deep in conversation.

Dotti was dressed in attractive evening attire, and Miss la Mer in a low-cut red lace evening dress.

Jean remarked wryly, "That man must have hypnotized her. He's holding her ring, and right over the water, too!"

As the girls edged closer, they heard Enrico say, "This ruby certainly is one of rare beauty."

"Yes, I adore it," Rosamunde la Mer remarked, taking the ring from him.

She was about to slip the ring back on her little finger when suddenly it fell from her grasp. Both she and Enrico tried to grab the piece of jewelry but missed it.

The singer gave a shriek as the ring fell into the ocean and cried out, "It's gone! My precious, priceless ruby is lost forever!"

CHAPTER V

Hypnotists at Work

As ROSAMUNDE la Mer sobbed hysterically, Louise and Jean Dana rushed toward her.

"Oh, why did I ever take my ring off!" the singer cried out in a choked voice.

Enrico Dotti patted her on the shoulder. "It's all my fault," he said. "I never should have asked you to take it off." Then he added in a practical tone, "But surely, Miss la Mer, the ring is insured. Such a valuable piece of jewelry must be."

The singer gave him a withering look. "What if it is?" she asked. "Money can't replace it. I had great sentimental attachment for that ring." She burst into tears again.

The Danas said that they had seen the accident and expressed their sympathy. The girls' comforting words and warm smiles seemed to make the woman feel better.

"Oh, I shouldn't act like a baby," she said. "But

the ring meant a good deal to me. It was a present from someone I loved dearly." Miss la Mer did not explain further.

All this time Enrico Dotti had been looking at the sisters with an expression of great annoyance. They suddenly realized they had broken up a tête-à-tête. Before the girls had a chance to apologize, the hypnotist said curtly, "I'll see you later, Miss la Mer," and stalked off.

The singer gazed after him vacantly and the sisters wondered if she had even heard what the man had said.

Presently Louise asked, "Miss la Mer, by any chance was the gem in your ring known as a winking ruby?"

Miss la Mer knit her brow and looked intently at Louise. "Winking ruby?" she repeated slowly. "No. But tell me, what does it mean?"

The Danas confessed that they did not know and only recently had heard the phrase.

Suddenly the singer caught her breath. "Come to think of it," she said, "I did hear one time about a fabulous jewel called the winking ruby. I had forgotten all about it."

"Can you tell us any more about the gem?" Jean prodded the woman eagerly.

Miss la Mer shook her head. "I can't recall any of the details. But that's the kind of brain I have. My mind is like an old attic—it has all kinds of things stored in the corners that come popping out unexpectedly."

The Danas smiled at this quaint expression, but Miss la Mer gave a deep sigh. She looked down into the green waters below her.

"Losing my ruby ring is like losing a friend," she said. "But I mustn't bother you girls with my sorrow. It's very nice of you to stay here and sympathize with me."

"We wish that we could be of help," Jean said, as the singer started to walk away.

"Before you go, Miss la Mer," Louise spoke up, "I'd like to ask you one more question. Do you know anyone named Carlo?"

"No, I don't—either professionally or otherwise. Sorry." Miss la Mer said good-by and walked off.

The sisters returned to their stateroom. Aunt Harriet and their school friends were dressed and the five went toward the dining room. On the way Jean told about the ruby ring which had been lost overboard.

Aunt Harriet gasped. "Oh, dear," she said, "I feel as if I were partly to blame. If I had only let you girls warn Miss la Mer about the ring, maybe she wouldn't have worn it."

Jean put an arm about Miss Dana. "Don't worry about that now, Aunty dear. As you often say to me 'No use crying over spilt milk.' "

When the group reached the large, mirrored dining room, they found that they had been assigned to the captain's table. Uncle Ned introduced them to the other guests seated at his table. These included Professor and Mrs. Rudolph Jensen. The professor was a distinguished-looking, white-haired man and his wife was an attractive woman with deep dimples.

The other couple was Dr. and Mrs. David Bronson. They were tall and dark and in the early thirties. As the soup course was being served, Captain Dana told his other guests that Dr. Bronson was a specialist in bone diseases. The physician was on his way to England to deliver a lecture before a medical society there.

"And Professor Jensen," Uncle Ned went on, "I understand that you have earned a couple of degrees by your study of old castles."

The charming old gentleman, who said he had recently retired from university teaching, chuckled. "I wish getting my degree years ago had been that easy," he said. "Actually my thesis was about dungeons in old European castles and their relation to various wars."

Louise and Jean were intrigued. The air of mystery surrounding such places was exactly what they liked to read about.

"Working on those old stories must have been like solving mysteries," said Louise, who was seated on the professor's left.

"Yes, it was," he answered. "Do you like mysteries?"

At this remark Captain Dana laughed heartily. He told the guests at the table that his nieces spent all the waking hours that they could spare trying to solve the mysteries they encountered.

Professor Jensen's eyes twinkled. "Then I think you'll like this story," he said. "In a ruined castle in Germany I came upon three connecting dungeons. This was most surprising because a dungeon usually has no access to any other room except a corridor. But openings had been hacked through.

"Previously," Dr. Jensen went on, "I had unearthed the fact that the castle had been shattered in the middle ages. This was during a siege by a neighboring baron who wanted to annex the land to his own. But though he won the battle, nothing which he planted on the stolen soil afterward ever grew. The reason remained a mystery."

As the professor stopped speaking, Mrs. Jensen smiled. "It remained a mystery until my husband solved it," she said proudly. "Go on, dear, and tell the girls the rest of the story."

"There's not much more to it," the professor said. "The baron whose castle was ruined had a friend, named Lenz, who was an alchemist. He carried on secret experiments in the empty dungeons, trying to make gold from various minerals.

"When it became evident during the siege that the baron could not hold out against his enemy,

Lenz promised to help him get even with the attacker but did not say how. The alchemist disappeared and was never heard from again.

"But through my own digging in those dungeons," Dr. Jensen said, "I discovered that there was a poison chemical in the stone walls which would kill any kind of plant life. I felt pretty sure Lenz had escaped the siege but had later come back secretly. Whenever the fields were planted by the conqueror, the alchemist would go out at night and sprinkle the poison chemical over the ground. Thus the crops never grew."

"What a weird story!" Doris spoke up.

"And what a warped kind of friendship!" Evelyn added.

Louise leaned toward the professor. "While you were digging in the ruins, did you come across anything else which helped you reach this conclusion?"

Dr. Jensen laughed and turned toward Captain Dana. "You didn't tell me I was going to be cross-examined," he teased. "I see that only the truth and nothing but the truth will satisfy these sleuthing nieces of yours."

"I'm afraid that's right," Uncle Ned replied with a laugh.

Professor Jensen explained that in one of the dungeons he had found some ancient parchments which had been cleverly concealed. The writing on them had been hard to decipher. But here and there was a clue which convinced him that he had hit upon the truth.

Jean remarked dreamily, "How I'd love to go poking around old dungeons!"

"Well, I hope you'll have a chance to do that someday," said Professor Jensen. "But be careful. Some of them are treacherous."

As the little dinner party was about to break up, the head steward came over to the table and handed Louise a note. Excusing herself, she opened it. It was from Enrico Dotti and invited Louise to come for a hypnotic session free of charge.

Puzzled, Louise passed the note to her uncle.

Captain Dana read the message and frowned. "I think you'd better not go, Louise," he said. "I don't like the idea of your being hypnotized."

His niece did not argue the point at the table. But later, after Jean had read the note, the girls followed the captain to his quarters. They told their uncle they felt sure that there was a special reason in back of Dotti's request.

"I'd like to find out what it is," said Louise. "I have a hunch it may concern Carlo."

"In what way?" Uncle Ned asked.

Louise told of the Dottis' strange actions when questioned about Carlo. "They may think *I* know something and want to find out what it is."

The captain grinned. "I see. And you hope to turn the tables and learn something from them.

Well, I doubt that you will. The hypnotists were recommended to the steamship company as persons above reproach, or they wouldn't be permitted to practice on board the *Balaska*."

Louise and Jean did not share their uncle's confidence but kept the thought to themselves. Aloud Louise said, "I understand a person needn't permit himself to be hypnotized. I'm sure that I can just pretend to be."

Captain Dana finally consented to her going for a session. "That is, on one condition," he said. "You must take Aunt Harriet and all the girls with you."

Louise agreed.

Uncle Ned wished her luck and the sisters hurried off. A few minutes later they were on their way to the Dottis' suite with Aunt Harriet, Evelyn, and Doris.

When they walked in, Enrico and his wife looked at the group with irritation. But a moment later both smiled and Enrico said:

"I am delighted, Miss Dana, that you have consented to have a free treatment. You are probably wondering why I made the offer. The answer is, frankly, that business has not been very good. On the trip over I had very few patients."

The hypnotist gave a hollow laugh. "After all, my wife and I must make a living. I thought perhaps you wouldn't mind being my subject tonight. When word spreads that the captain's niece was here, I'm sure that others will come too."

"You are now asleep!" the hypnotist intoned.

The man spoke convincingly and Louise pretended to be persuaded. "All right," she said. "I've never been hypnotized. What do I do?"

"Well, first of all, your friends will have to leave."

Aunt Harriet stepped forward. "No," she said firmly. "My niece is not of age. I'm responsible for what she does. I, at least, will have to stay here."

The Dottis looked at each other, then finally Enrico consented to everyone staying. He invited them into the next room. Here he donned his flowing red-and-gold robe and turban, then requested that the onlookers sit down. He led Louise to a large lounge chair and asked her to recline in it.

Louise did so. The hypnotist now moved forward and stared into the girl's eyes, telling her to look steadily at him. From his pocket he took a midget flashlight, turned it on, and began to beam the light round and round in a tiny circle.

Presently Louise's eyelids seemed to grow heavy and a few seconds later they closed. Jean became worried. Her sister had been so sure she could not be hypnotized and now apparently she *had* been! What might she tell under this state?

"You are now asleep," Enrico Dotti was intoning. "You are very peaceful and have nothing to be afraid of. You are a girl who loves to solve mysteries."

As he paused, Jean held her breath. What was coming next?

"You have many admirers," Enrico went on. "One of them sent you a snake to frighten you. Now tell me, whom do you suspect?"

For a moment Louise did not answer, then she said slowly, "It . . . must . . . have . . . been . . . Daniel!"

For a second Jean was startled. She was sure Louise did not know anyone named Daniel. Then she almost burst out laughing and relaxed. Louise was not in a hypnotic state at all. She had made up the answer!

"But Daniel used the name Carlo to mystify me," Louise murmured slowly. "I wonder who Carlo is."

As Louise said this, Jean watched the two hypnotists narrowly. Did she detect signs of relief?

The session continued for nearly ten minutes. The Dottis' questions were inconsequential and Louise's answers in no way revealing.

Lena Dotti went over very close to Louise. She looked down at the sleeping girl for a moment, then whispered something to her husband. At once he looked at Louise, then turned in alarm toward Aunt Harriet.

"Your niece is in a deeper trance than usual. There's nothing to worry about. But," he added, with a significant stare, "my wife and I must have absolute control with no interference in order to bring her to wakefulness."

Miss Dana had gone ash white. "You mean

Louise— Oh, perhaps we'd better get the doctor."

"That won't be necessary," Lena Dotti spoke up. "But go. Hurry, please!"

Evelyn and Doris left immediately. Aunt Harriet and Jean, in a quandary, paused. But knowing they could do nothing themselves, they decided to wait outside a few minutes and hurried into the corridor.

"This is dreadful," Miss Dana said, twisting her fingers nervously as she paced up and down.

Jean was still hoping that Louise was playing a part, and without them in the room, would learn something important from the Dottis. But her heart was thumping wildly with worry nevertheless.

"Maybe Louise won't wake up," said Evelyn, a tremble in her voice. "She might become an amnesia victim!"

"Let's wait a few minutes to see what happens," Jean suggested. "Then, if Louise doesn't come out, I'm going back inside."

Fearfully they stood at the door as the seconds ticked by.

CHAPTER VI

The Seaman's Clue

DORIS began to pace back and forth nervously in the corridor of the *Balaska*. Finally she whispered to Evelyn that they ought to find Captain Dana and bring him to the hypnotists' stateroom.

"I'll do it," said Evelyn and ran off.

Nervously Miss Dana pulled a handkerchief from her suit pocket and twisted it into a little ball. "I shouldn't have allowed Louise to go through with the hypnotist business."

Jean tried to appear calm, but never took her eyes off the door. Fervently she hoped that her sister would walk out unharmed! As minute after minute went by, however, Jean had to fight down a feeling of panic.

"Here comes your uncle," Doris cried in relief.

Captain Dana, with Evelyn, was striding along the corridor, a look of great concern on his face. The others knew that he would not wait for an invitation to enter the hypnotists' quarters. He would march in and demand an explanation!

But it was not necessary for him to do this. At that moment the door opened and Louise stepped into the hallway. She seemed to be all right. Seeing her family and friends she smiled.

"Thank goodness you're here!" exclaimed the three girls in unison.

"Are you all right?" Aunt Harriet asked her niece anxiously.

"If you're not," Uncle Ned said grimly, "those two inside are going to answer to me! I'll—"

He broke off and started toward the Dottis' door. Louise put a restraining hand on the captain's arm. "Really, Uncle Ned, I'm fine." She chuckled. "And I enjoyed being hypnotized. By the way, what did I say while I was asleep?"

The others looked at her in amazement.

Then Louise gave a big wink, and invited them all to come with her. "Let's talk about hypnotism," she said gaily.

Wondering what Louise had in mind, the Danas and their friends followed her to Uncle Ned's quarters. They seated themselves in the comfortable wicker chairs and waited for her to begin.

"Please don't look so worried, Aunt Harriet," she begged with a laugh. "I actually was never in a hypnotic state."

"What!" Doris exclaimed. "Even when you didn't move, you were only pretending?"

"That's right," said Louise. "I admit that at one time when Enrico Dotti was waving that flashlight around and staring at me, I started to feel drowsy."

Jean wagged her head. "Well, Sis," she said, "you certainly put on a good act. You had me almost convinced."

"I'll say she did," Evelyn spoke up. "I was scared out of my wits."

At this, Doris nodded vigorously in agreement. Then she begged, "Tell us what happened after we left the room."

Louise said she was sorry to have frightened the group. But the young sleuth had realized that she would never learn anything important from the Dottis while the others were in the room.

"So I pretended to go into a still deeper sleep," she explained. "Everything worked out perfectly. Of course I knew I was taking an awful chance," Louise admitted. "Incidentally, since I apparently did fool Enrico and Lena, I'd say they're very amateurish at this hypnotism business. I doubt that they've had any real training."

Captain Dana frowned. "In that case, this will be the Dottis' last trip on the *Balaska!* Well, go on with your story."

After the others had left the room, Louise said that Enrico and Lena had debated whether or not they should bring her out of the hypnotic state immediately. Lena had said no, that they should find out all they could first. Her husband had acceded.

"Then they asked me what the purpose of my trip to Europe was. I told them that people thought I was trying to solve a mystery, but that actually we girls had boy friends in England and that we were just going to have lots of fun sight-seeing with them."

Doris gave a great sigh. "I wish that were true!" she exclaimed. "Then what happened?"

Louise replied that the hypnotists wanted to know where else the Danas were going to travel and she had answered, "Wherever fancy leads us.

"But finally," Louise went on, "the couple got around to the big question. They asked me why we had quizzed them about Gino and Carlo. It took me a little longer to figure out how to throw them off the track on this one. But at last I told them: 'Well, Gino isn't married and my uncle knows of a wonderful girl named Cora Appel. My sister and I thought we might get them together, but now, since Gino is ill, I guess that's out of the question. I do wish he'd get well so we could arrange a meeting.' "

At this everyone in the room burst into laughter, and Jean said, "Applecore, of all people! How could you keep a straight face, Lou?"

Uncle Ned boomed, "Louise, I didn't know you had such imagination!"

Louise smiled and paused in her storytelling. As her listeners leaned forward expectantly, Evelyn urged, "Go on. Don't stop, please!"

"There's not much more," Louise replied. "They questioned me again about Carlo, but of course I insisted I didn't know anybody by that name. Then finally Lena said, 'We'd better bring this girl back to a conscious state. Her family may become suspicious.'

"They both began telling me that I was waking up and Enrico even tried some hocus-pocus gibberish. I almost gave myself away by laughing. Finally, when I thought it was the right moment, I opened my eyes and got up. The Dottis must have believed me, so here I am."

"I think you're simply wonderful!" cried Doris, rushing over to give Louise a bear hug.

Aunt Harriet was wiping away a few tears of relief. She said nothing, just smiled at her niece proudly.

Captain Dana suggested that the whole episode become a closed subject. "It might cause trouble if the Dottis ever hear that Louise was acting."

"Yes," said Jean. "They certainly were snoopy about our plans. I wonder why." Then she giggled. "Right now, thanks to you, Louise, the Dottis probably think we're the world's worst detectives! Let's let them continue to think so."

"All right," Louise agreed. "But I want to go on

with our sleuthing right away. Uncle Ned, I'd like
to question the crew about the snake, and about
Gino. When would be a good time?"

Captain Dana said that at the moment a movie
was being shown in the crew's recreation quarters.

"Suppose you and Jean come here at ten o'clock
and I'll take you down there. When the picture
is over, you can question the men."

At ten o'clock the sisters met their uncle and together they walked down to a lower deck. The
motion picture was about to end. As the lights were
turned on, Captain Dana arose and introduced his
nieces.

"They'd like to ask you a few questions," he
announced.

Louise inquired if any of the crew could give
her information which might help stir the violinist's
memory. "Or," she added, "did any of you ever
hear Gino refer to a winking ruby—or someone
named Carlo?"

But the men responded to her queries with a
murmur of "No's" and headshaking.

"I have one more question," Louise said. "You
may have heard that someone delivered a wicker
basket containing a snake to my sister's and my
cabin. Did any of you see a person with such a
basket?"

A young seaman stood up. "I can answer that
one," he stated. "When I was coming aboard, a
man stopped me and asked if I would do him a

favor. He said, 'I'm in a hurry. I'm supposed to deliver this basket to Misses Louise and Jean Dana in Room 326. Can you take it for me?' So I told him yes I would. I put it in your cabin, miss. I didn't know there was a snake in the basket— honest."

"I'm sure that you didn't," said Louise. "Will you please describe the man who handed you the basket."

"Well, there wasn't anything special about him," the seaman replied. "He did have red hair, though."

Louise's pulse quickened. Here was a real clue! Was the red-haired man she had seen on the dock named Carlo? Was he the person to whom Gino Marzi had referred? And most important of all, was it the Dottis to whom he had been signaling?

"Thank you very much," said Louise.

After Uncle Ned and the girls had left the recreation quarters, Jean whispered to her uncle that she thought there was enough suspicion against the hypnotists to have them watched.

"Why, they may even have the winking ruby in their possession!" she said excitedly. "Uncle Ned, would it be possible to have their rooms searched?"

Captain Dana patted his niece's shoulder. "Now calm down, my hearty," he said. "You're walking the plank blindfolded. I couldn't possibly have the Dottis' rooms searched without any concrete evidence. But I'll tell you what I'll do. I'll have the ship's detective keep an eye on them."

"You have a detective on board?" Jean asked with interest. "Oh, I'd love to meet him."

Captain Dana smiled. "No one on board but myself knows who this detective is. The steamship company engages a new one for each trip, so that none of the passengers can possibly spot him."

Louise laughed. "That's very clever, Uncle Ned," she said. "Maybe Jean and I would make more progress if no one knew we're sleuthing."

"Don't let that worry you," her uncle said. "I'm sure ninety-five percent of the people on board don't know it and the other five percent—except us—don't know what good detectives my nieces really are."

The girls chuckled and made mock bows. Then Louise said, "You know, Uncle Ned, the Dottis may be practicing hypnotism to cover up some racket they're mixed up in. If it's not on the ship, it may be in Europe or America."

Captain Dana smiled. "You girls are persistent, but it's no use. I refuse to take any chances. I'll notify the British police to watch the Dottis from the moment they disembark."

At breakfast the next morning Evelyn reminded the other girls that this was the day when the ping-pong tournament would begin. In the first match she and Jean would be partners against Louise and Doris. At ten o'clock the girls hurried on deck and were assigned to a table. There was a good-sized crowd on hand, with three other groups playing, two for singles matches and another for doubles.

"I feel lucky," Jean called across the net. "Here goes!" She sent a blazing serve which Doris missed.

Jean's play held at a high level throughout the three games. She and Evelyn won two of them and were told they would meet their next opponents, a bride and groom, early that afternoon.

As the game began, Louise and Doris watched it from the rail. The play was fast.

Presently Louise noticed Rosamunde la Mer walking toward the ping-pong area. Seeing Louise, the singer came up to her.

"Good afternoon," she said. "I'm glad I found you. I've just heard something that may be of great interest to you."

"Please tell me," said Louise. "But first, I'd like you to meet my friend, Doris Harland."

Miss la Mer acknowledged the introduction, then leaned close to Louise and whispered, "My gossipy room steward just told me that there's a woman on board named Mrs. Cracken. She has a ring very much like the one I lost."

"That *is* interesting," said Louise.

"Mrs. Cracken doesn't wear the ring," Miss la Mer continued. "The steward said he'd seen her looking at it rather furtively. She had taken it from a secret compartment in her jewel case."

Louise was intrigued by the story. "Did he say any more?" she asked.

The singer went on, "The steward said that the

ruby glinted so brightly it seemed to wink. That made me think of your question about the winking ruby. Well, I must hurry along now."

After thanking Miss la Mer and saying good-by, Louise became lost in thought. Maybe Mrs. Cracken was the person to whom the red-haired man on the dock had been signaling! And could her ruby be the one to which Gino Marzi had referred? Louise wondered.

CHAPTER VII

The Secret Compartment

LOUISE was snapped out of her reverie by the referee's shout of "Twenty-one!" The ping-pong match was over. Louise and Doris smiled broadly.

"The winners, Jean Dana and Evelyn Starr!" the referee announced, and the losers came around the table to shake their hands.

Louise and Doris rushed up to congratulate them. The winners laughed and Jean remarked, "Well, we're still in the tournament. I wonder who our next opponents will be."

The four girls went into the lounge to look at the draw sheet on the wall. Another doubles match had just been concluded and the winners' names were being entered in the next bracket. When Evelyn saw the names Laura Goodwin and Susan Powers, she groaned good-naturedly.

"These are the people we'll have to play tomorrow morning, Jean. And I hear they're among the best doubles players on board ship."

Jean smiled. "Evelyn, if you play as well in the next match as you did today, we'll mow 'em down!"

When Louise told her, a little later, about the conversation between herself and Rosamunde la Mer, Jean whistled. "I hope we can meet this Mrs. Cracken. I'd like to see that winking ruby ring."

"I was thinking the same thing," Louise replied with a smile. "Let's ask Uncle Ned to introduce us."

They found Captain Dana in the office of his quarters. He was interested in the story, but annoyed with the room steward for gossiping.

"I'll have him reprimanded," he said sternly. "Not about the ring, for he unwittingly may have done you a favor. But on gossiping in general." He picked up his phone and called Mrs. Cracken's stateroom. She answered at once. To Uncle Ned's request that he would like to call with his nieces, she replied effusively:

"Oh, how perfectly charming! This is a great honor, Captain. I'll expect you about a half hour before dinner."

"One thing sure," Louise remarked, as her uncle hung up, "Mrs. Cracken doesn't seem worried about why we're calling. She certainly didn't act startled, or as if she had any knowledge to conceal."

Captain Dana's eyes twinkled. "Well, my heart-ies," he said, "I have a feeling that this time you're off course."

When the girls met their uncle later, they looked lovely in their long evening dresses. Louise's was pale green and Jean wore a red-and-white checked one.

Captain Dana knocked on the door of Mrs. Cracken's stateroom. It was opened by a slightly plump woman of medium height. She wore an attractive pale-blue brocade evening dress.

"Do come in," she invited, smiling at the callers.

Mrs. Cracken was very gracious, but the Danas soon found that she talked incessantly. Within five minutes after their arrival, the girls and their uncle had learned that she was a widow, had had three husbands from whom she had inherited money, had traveled a great deal and did not believe in getting in her children's way. Also, although she was an American, the woman thought that Paris was the only place in the world to live!

"You're wearing beautiful and unusual jewelry, Mrs. Cracken," Jean remarked admiringly when the woman finally paused. "I suppose that since you travel a great deal, you bought these lovely pieces in various parts of the world."

"Yes, I have," Mrs. Cracken agreed. She arose and went to open the door to the corridor. "It's rather close in here, don't you think?"

Louise, concerned that the conversation might

be overheard by anyone in the passageway, suggested that it might be just as pleasant if the air conditioner were turned on and the door kept closed.

Mrs. Cracken shook her head violently, opened the door, and hooked it back. "I hate air conditioners! They give me a stuffy nose!"

Turning back, she went to the bureau and opened the top drawer. Rummaging under some lingerie, she brought out a large red velvet box. Mrs. Cracken held it open so that her visitors could see the contents. The girls ohed and ahed as they peered inside.

"More beautiful jewelry!" exclaimed Jean.

"I adore every piece," Mrs. Cracken remarked, as she lifted up what proved to be a false bottom. Beneath was a ring box. Taking this out, the woman opened it.

"Look at this," she said.

The three visitors found themselves staring at the most gorgeous ruby ring they had ever seen.

"Oh!" Louise gasped. "I've never seen anything so exquisite!"

Jean and Uncle Ned, too, expressed their admiration.

"Mrs. Cracken," Louise said, "is this, by any chance, called a winking ruby?"

She and Jean watched the woman intently to see if she showed any sign of alarm. They could detect none, and Mrs. Cracken replied immediately:

"If it is, I was never told that. I recently purchased the ring in New York." She gave a satisfied chuckle. "I got it at a real bargain, too."

Reaching into the bureau drawer, she drew out her handbag. Mrs. Cracken thumbed through its jumbled contents and brought out a bill of sale. She showed it to her visitors, who blinked rapidly. Five thousand dollars!

As Mrs. Cracken returned the paper to her purse, she went on, "This business of having to show bills of sale when you enter a country is all tommyrot. Why can't a person go from place to place without being bothered by customs? Now, Captain Dana, couldn't you do something about it?"

Uncle Ned was taken by surprise. Then, as usually happened when he found himself in a ridiculous situation, the captain roared with laughter.

"I'd like to oblige you, ma'am, but I'm afraid even an international lawyer couldn't decide that problem."

He cleared his throat and arose, indicating that the call was at an end. Secretly Louise and Jean felt that their uncle wanted to escape before he might be asked any more impossible questions!

"I must hurry off," he said, "but you girls stay a bit longer if you like. I'll see you at dinner. Very pleasant call, Mrs. Cracken." He strode off.

"We should go, too," said Jean, feeling that the girls had learned all they could.

She and Louise told Mrs. Cracken that they were delighted to have met her and hoped she would enjoy the voyage.

"But don't you think," Louise added, "that you're taking a chance leaving your jewelry in the cabin? Perhaps you ought to put the case in the ship's safe?"

"I suppose I should. But I love them so I want to keep them with me and look at them often."

Suddenly she grasped Louise's arm. "That winking ruby you mentioned!" she exclaimed. "I *do* remember once when I was in Italy I heard that phrase used about a gem."

"*A gem!*" the Danas thought. This definitely established the winking ruby as a gem!

"Oh me," said Mrs. Cracken petulantly, "I wish I could remember more about the stone. Maybe I could buy it!"

"I wish too," said Louise, "that you could recall more about it. A winking ruby sounds fascinating. I'd like to see one."

Secretly she was excited. Here was another clue! Italy this time—the homeland of the Marzis! Louise turned toward her sister to find her near the doorway, staring into the corridor. Suddenly Jean called, "Good-by, Mrs. Cracken," and left hurriedly.

"I wonder what Jean is up to," Louise thought as she shook hands with Mrs. Cracken and stepped into the corridor.

She caught sight of her sister hurrying up the hallway. Ahead of her was Lena Dotti. Puzzled, Louise quickly caught up to Jean.

"What happened?" she asked.

Jean said that Mrs. Dotti had been standing outside Mrs. Cracken's door. "I couldn't tell whether she was eavesdropping or just passing by. Anyway, I thought I'd better do a little eavesdropping of my own."

Mrs. Dotti entered her own cabin and closed the door. Louise and Jean paused outside and listened. There was not a sound from within.

Jean said in a low voice, "Either Enrico Dotti isn't there or his wife didn't learn anything about Mrs. Cracken's ruby ring to pass along to him."

"Perhaps she wasn't eavesdropping," Louise suggested. "Let's go!"

The Danas started toward their own deck to pick up Aunt Harriet, Evelyn, and Doris. Halfway there, they were suddenly thrown off balance and slammed against one side of the corridor. In a moment the ship swung the other way and the girls found themselves clutching the opposite wall.

"A little roll!" exclaimed Louise, catching her breath.

"A big one!" said Jean as she was thrown back to the other side. "I guess we've run into stormy weather."

Though the ship continued to pitch and roll, the girls soon found their sea legs and were able to sway from side to side with the motion of the *Balaska,* as Captain Dana had taught them as children.

"Aunt Harriet won't like this," Louise prophesied.

Entering Miss Dana's cabin, the sisters found their aunt lying on her bed. She looked very pale. "I—I don't feel well, girls. Hope you are doing better."

"We're all right," Jean assured her. "Is there anything we can get you?"

Miss Dana shook her head. "Thanks, no. I'll just lie here. I'll be all right. But I don't feel like eating."

Louise and Jean went to the neighboring stateroom. Doris and Evelyn, though they were not lying down, declared they were beginning to feel a bit squeamish.

"I don't think we'll be having dinner," Evelyn said with a grimace.

As Louise and Jean walked out, they decided that some fresh air would keep them from feeling ill!

"Let's walk outside," Louise suggested.

When they reached the wind-swept deck, they were fascinated by the stormy sea. The water was a leaden gray. The waves were high and crested with crashing whitecaps.

As the Danas walked, they came to the closed-off section where the ping-pong tables had been.

All the equipment had been taken inside, as well as the deck chairs. No one was around, but a moment later they saw an elderly man clutching the rail and moving in their direction.

"That's Professor Jensen," said Louise. "Maybe we can help him."

The two girls tried to hurry toward the professor. They had almost reached him when the ship gave a tremendous lurch. The two girls were thrown off balance and sprawled onto the deck.

At the same instant, Professor Jensen lost his grasp on the railing and pitched forward. His head hit a steel stanchion, and he fell to the deck, unconscious!

CHAPTER VIII

Another Hurricane Accident

GENTLY the Dana girls chafed Professor Jensen's wrists and temples. He did not return to consciousness, however, and suddenly the girls noticed that the elderly man had suffered a fairly deep gash on the side of his head.

"He needs medical attention," said Louise. "We'd better carry him to the doctor's office."

"Yes," Jean agreed, "but it's going to be hard work on a rolling ship."

By this time the *Balaska* was tossing more wildly than ever and the wind had risen to a howling gale. The girls' hair streamed out straight from their heads and their full evening skirts ballooned.

"Well, here goes," said Louise. She put her arms under those of the professor, while Jean held his legs.

It was a tremendous struggle to reach the door to the lounge and impossible to open it while carrying their burden. Finally the girls were forced to lay the unconscious figure down. Then, while Jean held the door open, Louise dragged the professor through.

"I wish we had a stretcher," said Louise. "But there's no one in sight to help us find one."

"I think," Jean decided, "that the way this ship is rocking, it would be safer for us to carry the professor across our shoulders."

"I agree," said Louise.

Standing one behind the other, the Danas lifted the limp form. They placed his chest on Louise's right shoulder and his knees across Jean's left shoulder. They held him tightly, then started off once more. To keep from bumping into the sides of the corridor and further injuring the victim, Louise put out her left hand to steady herself and Jean her right. In this way they finally reached the office of the ship's doctor.

"I hope he's here." Jean heaved a sigh.

But there was no response to their knock. Louise opened the door and they walked in. Neither the physician nor his nurse was there. They laid the professor on a bunk, then Jean said:

"What do you think we'd better do?"

For answer, Louise pulled up the guard rail at the edge of the bunk, so that their patient would not roll off. Then she opened the medicine closet. Locating a bottle of smelling salts, she took it out and held the bottle under the professor's nose.

"I hope this revives him," she said, worried.

Jean, meanwhile, had found some antiseptic and bandage on a table. She cleansed the wound on the elderly man's head. Then, as she was covering the cut with a bandage, the professor opened his eyes.

Dazedly he asked. "Where am I?"

"In the doctor's office," said Jean.

The professor looked around. "Who brought me here?"

Louise explained and said the physician probably would return soon. As she finished speaking, Dr. Stanley walked in. He looked at the trio in surprise.

"Oh, hello," he said. "Another patient? I'm sorry I wasn't here. Had to go out on an emergency, and my nurse is still with the patient."

Professor Jensen smiled. "I guess these girls have me fixed up, Doc," he said. "Cheated you out of a job."

The physician laughed, made an examination of his own, then praised the Danas for their efficient work. "I couldn't have done better myself," he said.

The professor looked at the girls. "If you young ladies could just help me to my cabin—" He chuckled. "You're sure-footed enough to climb the snow-covered Alps with an earthquake going on!"

Laughing, Jean said, "The *Balaska* certainly feels that way right now!"

"I'm sorry," said Dr. Stanley, "but I think you'd

better stay here in sick bay overnight, Professor."

The elderly man did not argue. He asked the physician to notify his wife of the accident, then he turned to the Danas.

"Thank you for your trouble in looking after me." He said that in all his travels he had not been through such a storm. "Why, this is a real hurricane. You girls had better go to your stateroom and lie down. It's not safe to be walking around, as I can testify."

The sisters decided to take his advice. As soon as they left the doctor's office, the girls started for their own cabin. Halfway there, they met Mrs. Cracken, who was clutching her velvet jewel case.

"Oh, Mrs. Cracken!" Louise cried out, as the woman lurched with a bang into the wall.

"This is dreadful! Perfectly dreadful!" Mrs. Cracken complained. "This ship is going to sink any minute!"

"Oh, I'm sure it's not," said Louise reassuringly. "But why are you out of your cabin?"

"I'm going to the purser's office," Mrs. Cracken replied excitedly. "I want to put my jewels in the safe before the ship sinks."

Despite the gravity of the situation, the Danas were amused at the flighty woman's reasoning. Why bother putting the jewels in the safe if the ship were going down? They noticed that she was wearing several expensive rings. What was she going to do with them?

"I'm ill—so ill," wailed Mrs. Cracken almost hysterically. Suddenly she thrust the jewel case into Jean's hands. "Please take this to the purser for me. I can't go another step."

"I'll be very glad to," Jean replied. "But first do you want us to help you back to your stateroom?"

"No, no!" the woman cried. "Just hurry. Get my precious jewels into the safe immediately before we sink."

At this moment Louise happened to look over Mrs. Cracken's shoulder. Not far behind her stood Enrico Dotti, who was wearing dark trousers and a white dinner jacket. Now the hypnotist dashed forward and started to take the velvet jewel case from Jean.

"I'll do the errand for Mrs. Cracken," he offered suavely. "You two girls had better get to your cabin before you're injured."

Jean pulled back and held the precious box tightly. In a firm tone she told Enrico that she and her sister would do the errand.

With a malevolent glare the hypnotist said icily, "Very well. I only wanted to be helpful. I was going there myself and thought I might save you the trouble." He turned to Mrs. Cracken, as if trying to obtain her consent to his offer.

"Oh, Mr. Dotti," she said coyly, "please help me to my room instead. I need a good strong man to keep me from falling down. It's not far."

Relieved, the Danas left the couple and hurried

The beautiful ring rolled out of sight.

toward the stairway which led down to the purser's office. By this time it seemed as if the ship were not only rolling and lurching but pitching from front and back at the same time. It was almost impossible to walk and the girls found themselves slipping and sliding at every step.

"It's going to be rough getting down these stairs," Louise remarked as they reached the broad, red-carpeted steps leading to the lower deck.

She grasped the railing on the left side. Jean took the one on the right, holding the jewel box firmly under her left arm. The girls descended slowly, swaying at each step.

Suddenly the *Balaska* gave a tremendous dip forward. Jean was swung around with such force that the jewel box slipped from beneath her arm and crashed to the stairway. It opened and all the jewelry inside flew in various directions! The beautiful ruby ring rolled down the stairway and out of sight.

"Oh, my goodness!" Jean cried out.

She and Louise hurried down the steps, as fast as they dared, to gather up the rings, pins, and necklaces. At this instant they became aware of someone else directly behind them. Turning, they saw that it was Enrico Dotti.

"Maybe now you'll let me help you," he said sarcastically. "I saw the accident."

Enrico found a pearl earring in a crevice of the

stairway, then a small diamond brooch. He handed them to Jean. She thanked him and dropped them into the jewel box.

Louise kept hoping she would find the ruby ring before he did. She began to search intently around the foot of the steps. But the next moment Enrico Dotti held up the ring.

"Beautiful, isn't it?" he asked, as he dropped the gem into the jewel box.

Without waiting for a reply, he walked across to the purser's office. Dotti spoke to Mr. Wingate, then went back up the stairway.

Meanwhile, Louise and Jean continued to search the stairway and floor thoroughly to make sure that all of Mrs. Cracken's jewelry had been found. Finally Jean closed the lid of the box and they walked over to the purser's counter. She explained that the Danas were depositing the jewel case for Mrs. Cracken and they would like a receipt for it.

As Mr. Wingate made one out, he remarked, "I'm surprised that you girls aren't in your cabin. Better watch out for a broken arm or leg!"

"We will," said Louise. "We're going to our room as soon as we deliver this receipt."

On the way Louise observed that they seemed to be the only passengers around. "And to tell you the truth," she confessed, "I'm getting tired of battling my way about."

When they reached Mrs. Cracken's cabin, they

were amazed to see that the door was open. Then they recalled that the woman had found it stuffy inside and did not like air conditioning.

The Danas walked in. Mrs. Cracken was on the bed asleep, her arms lying outside the sheet which covered her. They noticed at once that the beautiful rings the woman had been wearing were not on her fingers. The sisters looked at each other, the same thought entering their minds. Had Mrs. Cracken perhaps been robbed?

Louise decided to find out and awakened her. "We brought your receipt, Mrs. Cracken," she said. "By the way, what did you do with the rings you were wearing?"

Mrs. Cracken flung up her hands. The next moment she reached under her pillow, then tossed it onto the floor. Raising up, she stared at the spot where the pillow had been.

"I put them here," she said. "Right here."

The rings were not there now, nor had they fallen to the floor.

CHAPTER IX

Game Strategy

"WE'LL report the theft of your rings to my uncle, Mrs. Cracken," Jean offered.

"No, no!" the woman cried out. She groaned and fell back on the bed, putting both hands over her eyes. "That would only start a lot of trouble, and I dislike publicity. It doesn't matter about the rings. They were just cheap ones, anyway."

Louise and Jean were taken aback by this announcement. They did not believe Mrs. Cracken —the gems had been too beautiful not to be valuable. The girls concluded that she was afraid of being harmed should the theft be investigated.

"If that's the way you wish it, we'll say nothing about the matter," promised Jean reluctantly. "And I hope you'll feel better soon."

She and Louise turned to leave. Mrs. Cracken faced toward the porthole against which rain and sea water were pounding, and began to moan again.

"Oh, I feel terrible. Everything's wrong! Go away, girls! Please go away!"

The Danas, sensing they could do nothing for her, decided to leave. By now they had lost all interest in dinner and decided to go to bed. The sooner they could reach their cabin the happier they would be!

The ship was rolling and pitching more than ever and Louise and Jean wondered, as they made their way along, if they could possibly reach their stateroom without being injured. Once the sisters actually got down and crawled in order to avoid being slammed against the corridor wall.

"At last!" sighed Louise in relief as she unlocked the door to 326. It was not until then that Jean realized she had forgotten to give Mrs. Cracken the receipt for her jewel case.

"I just *can't* go back there now!" she wailed.

"I should say not," Louise agreed. "Tomorrow will do. Anyway, I think we can take better care of that receipt right now than Mrs. Cracken could."

Jean opened her purse, which was in the top drawer of her bureau, and slipped the receipt inside. Then both girls, after struggling into pajamas, lay down on their beds and pulled up the safety boards at the sides.

At this moment the storm seemed to reach the

height of its fury. Everything loose in the room was thrown out of position. The flower vase jumped from its rack on the bureau and crashed to the floor. The fruit scattered and landed hard against the walls.

"Oh, the fruit is ruined," Louise said, "and I haven't even written Ken to thank him for it!"

"I haven't thanked Chris, either," Jean confessed. "But we can do it before we land and send the letters airmail."

After that, conversation ceased. The sisters, luckily not seasick, were fascinated by the storm and the way the sturdy *Balaska* was riding it out. Louise and Jean knew that during all these hours their uncle had been on the bridge. In heavy storms he always insisted upon navigating the ship himself.

"Good old Uncle Ned!" was the thought in both girls' minds as they finally fell asleep, with complete trust that the captain would bring his ship safely through the storm.

By morning the *Balaska* had sailed beyond the hurricane area. The sky was blue, the sun shone warmly, and the ocean was calm. Smiling, Jean looked across the room at her sister who was just awakening.

" 'Morning, Sis," she said. "Boy, am I starved!"

Louise giggled. "Me too! I could eat a sea horse!"

They dressed quickly in white sports dresses,

then tapped on Aunt Harriet's door. She opened it promptly and kissed the girls affectionately.

"Are you feeling better this morning?" Louise asked her aunt.

Miss Dana smiled. "Fit as a bosun and all ready to pipe a signal. Shall we go to the dining room, girls?"

Her nieces laughed. "You've really gone nautical, Aunty," Louise told her.

Doris and Evelyn were ready and said they had recovered completely from their *mal de mer*. As the group started for the dining room, Louise and Jean told of their adventures the night before.

"My goodness!" Aunt Harriet exclaimed. "Accidents, thefts—what are you going to get into next?"

"A solution," quipped Jean, then added, "I wonder how Professor Jensen is."

To their delight he was at the table and assured them that he was feeling quite all right. Chuckling, he said to Miss Dana, "This patch on my head is evidence of your nieces' kindness to me last evening."

"Yes," Mrs. Jensen spoke up, "you girls were very brave." She smiled. "And went way beyond the call of duty."

The sisters blushed at the praise and changed the subject to the ping-pong tournament. "Jean and Evelyn have a hard match to play this morning," Louise told the others.

"We all wish you luck," said Aunt Harriet.

At ten o'clock the four girls went to the enclosed deck where the singles games were already in progress. Jean and Evelyn met their opponents, Laura Goodwin and Susan Powers, and the game began. The score seesawed back and forth with first one side ahead, then the other. Laura and Susan sent low drives which bounced far back. Jean and Evelyn found themselves missing too many of them.

"If we're going to win this match," Jean told herself, "we'll have to use a little strategy."

She began making the same kind of shots their opponents were hitting. Then, just when Susan and Laura had come to expect them, she suddenly dropped one gently over the net. Jean and Evelyn won the point.

This change of attack baffled the other two players, and in the last game the Starhurst girls won by a score of twenty-two to twenty!

"Our congratulations!" the losers called and came to shake hands with Jean and Evelyn.

"You're great!" Laura praised them.

"I hope you win the tournament doubles!" Susan Powers added.

"Thanks. You can bet we'll try!" Jean laughed.

Among the other winners were two boys, John Sampson and Joe Roberts. They were traveling with a group from a boys' school that planned to spend the summer in France.

"We're bicycling through the chateau country," John explained.

After talking with the Danas and their friends for a while, they introduced two of their friends, Cricky and Howie. The four couples spent the balance of the morning together.

"How about going to the dance with us this evening?" Joe suggested as lunchtime approached. The girls readily accepted and made arrangements to meet at nine o'clock.

Then the Danas returned to their staterooms to freshen up for luncheon. Jean suddenly snapped her fingers in dismay.

"Louise, I forgot all about giving Mrs. Cracken her receipt for the jewel box. I must take it to her at once."

Jean opened her purse to get it. Not seeing the slip of paper, she dumped the contents of the bag onto the bureau. The receipt was gone!

"But how could anyone get in here except Archie?" she exclaimed. "And I'm sure he didn't take it. *Now* what will I do?"

At that moment Aunt Harriet knocked on the door and came into the room. After hearing what had happened, she began to laugh.

"I'm sorry that you had such a scare, Jean. Mrs. Cracken came for the receipt this morning and I had Archie let me in here. I rummaged around until I found the paper."

Jean sighed in relief.

As the group walked to the dining room, the girls chatted gaily with Aunt Harriet about the boys they had met.

"I'm glad you found such nice new friends," she remarked. "To be truthful, I was beginning to think this trip would be all work and no play for you!"

That evening the girls wore pretty silk dresses and enjoyed themselves immensely. Their partners were excellent dancers and all had a good sense of humor.

At one point John and Louise walked out on deck for some fresh air. During their conversation he remarked that he had heard she was an amateur sleuth.

The boy grinned. "I'd better be careful not to let you know about any of my school escapades."

Louise laughed. "I may like to solve mysteries," she said, "but I'm not a jailer!" Then she became serious. "By the way, John, have you heard any of the passengers talking about someone named Carlo?"

"No, I haven't," John replied thoughtfully. "But it's a strange coincidence that you should mention that. An aunt of mine came over on the *Balaska* recently. She was telling me about the violinist Gino Marzi. I understand he was taken ill on the last trip."

"Yes," said Louise.

"My aunt," John went on, "enjoyed Mr. Marzi's playing very much and often discussed music with him. One day he commented on some jewelry she was wearing and mentioned that he had a relative, named Carlo, who was an expert jewelry craftsman."

Louise caught her breath. "How interesting! Did your aunt find out where this Carlo lived?"

"No, she didn't," John answered. "She said that almost as soon as he had told her about Carlo, Mr. Marzi acted embarrassed and had quickly changed the subject."

"Then you don't know," said Louise, "whether Carlo was this person's first or last name?"

"No, I don't. Sorry. Well, shall we dance again?"

They returned to the rest of the group and it was after midnight when the girls and their escorts said good night. Before going to bed, the Danas stopped in Doris and Evelyn's stateroom for a chat. They discussed what a wonderful evening they had had, and Louise told the others of the latest clue about Carlo.

"Oh, that's great!" said Jean.

Suddenly Doris wagged her finger at Louise. "Ken Scott had better watch out, or one John Sampson will be joining the Dana Detective Agency!"

Evelyn giggled. "That's right. I think I'll write to Chris and tell him he'd better change schools and take an FBI course next fall or he'll lose out!"

Before the Danas had a chance to retort to this teasing, Uncle Ned knocked and walked into the room. "Well, my hearties, I thought I'd come to say good night, but," he added with a worried frown, "I have some disturbing information for my nieces. I've just had a message about Gino Marzi."

CHAPTER X

Accused!

FEARFULLY Louise asked her uncle, "Has something happened to Gino Marzi?"

"No. It's not that."

Jean asked excitedly, "Has his memory been restored?"

"I wish that were so," Captain Dana replied. "Gino is better—he has gained strength and is really in good physical health now. But he is still suffering from amnesia."

The captain went on to say that he had talked with Gino's doctor by radiotelephone. "A mysterious letter came to the hospital for Gino. He gave it to the physician because he could not understand it. The letter was unsigned and undated. It had been postmarked in New York City the day the *Balaska* sailed."

"What did the letter say?" Louise asked.

"It was a threatening message," Uncle Ned

stated. "The writer accused Gino of pretending to have lost his memory and hiding away to avoid sending money that he owed. The man warned that if Gino didn't 'kick in' the money fast, his family would be harmed."

"Why, how perfectly dreadful!" Doris exclaimed. "Captain Dana, do you think Gino Marzi could be mixed up in some racket?"

"Yes, I believe he is," Uncle Ned answered. "But not because he wants to be. I still believe Gino is a fine young man and completely honest. No doubt unscrupulous persons have some hold over him, so he is under compulsion to pay them money." He turned to his nieces. "This complicates your mystery, my lassies, I'm afraid."

Louise told her uncle that she had learned Carlo was a relative of Gino Marzi's.

The captain raised his eyebrows in surprise. "Now, that *is* a valuable clue," he said. "It's my guess that Carlo is a very close relative, too—since Gino was so fearful for his safety."

"And Carlo's an expert jewelry craftsman," Louise added. "This must mean he's connected in some way with the winking ruby."

Evelyn asked the others if they thought Gino Marzi's mother and sister had disappeared because of the racket Gino and Carlo were in. "If they did," she added, "you may never find them."

But the Danas refused to become discouraged, and Jean said, "We've gathered a lot of good clues in a surprisingly short time. I have a hunch that once we fit the pieces of this puzzle together, we'll solve the mystery in a hurry."

"I certainly hope so," said Louise. "I bet Gino's memory would be restored if Carlo and the winking ruby could be saved."

"I agree with you," Jean replied.

"Well, time to turn in," said Captain Dana. He kissed his nieces and strode to the door. "Sleep well, and if I don't see you girls at breakfast, the best of luck to you, Jean and Evelyn, in your ping-pong tournament."

"Thanks, Uncle Ned! We'll need it!"

Presently the sisters said good night to their friends and went to their cabin. Just before turning out the lights, Jean remarked to her sister:

"Tomorrow's ping-pong games will be tough ones."

"Mm—yes," Louise murmured sleepily, "John Sampson and Joe Roberts are excellent players." She chuckled. "Maybe you and Evelyn should rate a special handicap!"

"No, thanks," said Jean. "We'll fight it through."

The following morning a large crowd had gathered to watch the finals of both the doubles and singles ping-pong tournaments. Good-natured banter was mixed with wishes for success to the two groups of players.

The doubles contest was to be two out of three games. Jean and Evelyn faced John and Joe across the long table and soon the four settled down to a fast and furious exchange. There was a steady *tap-tap* of ball against paddles. The first game was won by the boys. In the next, the girls played adroitly and came out the victors.

The audience began to clap and cheer. The third game was a vital one to both sides!

"You can do it, Jean and Evelyn! Don't let those boys beat you!" cried a group of college girls traveling together.

"Ho! You just watch!" John's friend Howie called out. "John's the best backhand ping-ponger in the United States!"

As the game progressed, the score rapidly see-sawed. But it finally became evident that John was indeed a master at the sport. There was a hush as the last points were reached. Finally the game was over and the referee called out:

"Winners John Sampson and Joe Roberts!"

When the applause died down, the girls shook hands with their opponents and congratulated them.

"Sorry we had to beat you," said John.

Joe grinned. "Guess we didn't give you sleuths enough time to figure out our mysterious shots! What say we plan a return engagement after we get back to the States?"

"Agreed," said Jean.

Doris Harland was somewhat upset. Her friends had fought so gallantly she had wanted them to win. But her look of disappointment changed to a smile when the prizes were presented. There were good-sized silver cups for the two boys and a pair for the girls not much smaller!

Jean and Evelyn were pleased, and Evelyn remarked, "These are really more our size, anyway!"

The rest of the voyage was extremely pleasant for the Danas and their friends. No new clues turned up in regard to the mystery of Carlo or the ruby. According to Captain Dana, the ship's detective had learned nothing suspicious about the Dottis or anyone else on board.

"But I've arranged for the English police to have a man trail the hypnotists after they go ashore," Uncle Ned told his nieces. He chuckled. "I guess you girls will have enough to do on the mystery in Florence to keep you busy."

On the last night aboard, everyone dressed in evening clothes to attend the captain's gala dinner. Aunt Harriet, her nieces told her proudly, looked particularly attractive in a powder-blue lace gown.

When the four Starhurst friends, wearing pretty contrasting pastel dresses, entered the dining room they gazed around admiringly. Festive decorations, which included balloons of many colors, dangled from the chandeliers and side lights. Paper hats and various kinds of merrymakers had been provided for each diner.

The Danas were especially intrigued by a display near the entrance to the dining room. Several chefs in tall white hats stood behind a long table on which were the most beautiful and elaborate desserts the girls had ever seen—huge blocks of colored ices carved in the shapes of fish and sailing ships. There were large cakes molded into castles, merry-go-rounds and, most gorgeous of all, a tropical garden.

"Oh—they're too lovely to eat!" declared Doris.

"Yes," Louise agreed. "Did those chefs make the cakes?" she asked Uncle Ned as the group seated themselves at his table.

"That's right," he replied. "They are artists as well as topnotch chefs."

"This trip has been so wonderful," Evelyn spoke up dreamily. "I feel like Alice in Wonderland. I hate to think it will all come to an end tomorrow morning."

Captain Dana smiled. "That's the best test of whether or not a person has had a good time," he remarked philosophically. Then he chuckled. "You know, no matter how many times I make the trip I get that same feeling myself."

"At least we still have a European adventure ahead of us," said Evelyn.

After the festivities were over, the passengers went to their staterooms to pack. A notice had gone out for all luggage, except hand pieces, to be ready for collection by midnight.

After their bags had been taken away by Archie and the girls were ready for bed, Louise said, "Let's get up early, so we can be on deck when we first come in sight of land."

"Fine. We'd better get to sleep right now!"

Soon after sunrise, the two travelers donned tailored dresses and scarves. They went outside and stood at the rail, watching excitedly as the outermost tip of England came into view.

"Oh, there's Land's End," Jean bubbled, as she gazed at the rocky shore line.

Aunt Harriet and the other girls joined them. A few minutes later they went to the dining room for an early breakfast, then hurried back on deck to watch as the *Balaska* sailed along the more densely populated section of the island. Various types of boats were anchored along the English Channel and there was an exchange of hand waving and picture taking. Finally the *Balaska* reached Southampton and was moored.

"We can stay on deck," Jean told Doris and Evelyn as the gangplank was put in place. "Uncle Ned will be among the last to leave the ship."

Passengers began to debark. Among the first to get off were Enrico and Lena Dotti. They said good-by to no one and hurried away quickly into the crowd. Louise and Jean strained their eyes for a trace of some detective who might be following them. But in the swarm of people they could not spot any man who they thought might be the one.

The girls turned their attention to a huge crane which was operated from shore and swung down into the depths of the hold. It brought out huge boxes, crates, and netted loads of baggage.

"And here comes a truck!" exclaimed Evelyn unbelievingly, as the huge vehicle was hoisted up and set on the dock.

Presently the Dana girls strolled into the lobby of the purser's office. They were just in time to see Mrs. Cracken turn in her receipt and receive her velvet jewel case. At once the woman opened it to gaze at her gems.

"Oh, I'm so glad the ship didn't sink," she said to Mr. Wingate.

A moment later she held up the ruby ring. As the Danas came closer they saw a startled look cross her face. Suddenly she gave a shriek and cried out:

"This isn't my ring! This is a cheap imitation!"

Amazed, Louise and Jean rushed to the woman's side. Mrs. Cracken looked at them blankly for a moment. Then, realizing who they were, she pointed a finger at the girls.

"You're responsible for this!" she exclaimed in a loud voice. "You've stolen my priceless ruby ring!"

The Danas were thunderstruck! And they realized that it would be difficult to prove their innocence. They had carried the jewel case to the purser's office themselves!

CHAPTER XI

A Warning

THE DANAS were too stunned by Mrs. Cracken's accusation to answer at once. But finally Jean found her voice.

"Of course we didn't take your ruby ring!" she said indignantly.

"But it's gone," Mrs. Cracken insisted. She held up a ring which looked very much like her valuable one. "This is a cheap imitation, I tell you! If you girls didn't substitute it, who did?"

"We don't know," Louise spoke up evenly. "And we don't like to accuse anybody. However, there is something I think we should tell you."

She related the story of their experience on the stairway during the hurricane and how the jewelry had scattered when the box opened.

"Mr. Dotti," Louise continued, "happened to be nearby and helped us pick up the jewelry. He found the ruby ring and gave it to me to put back in the box. I only glanced at it, so I couldn't say whether the ring was your original or not."

Mrs. Cracken's face grew red with fury. "You're saying that to cover up your own carelessness," she said in a high voice. "Mr. Dotti is a fine man. I had several treatments from him and he did me a world of good. Don't you dare accuse him of being a thief!"

"I'm not. Somebody else might have done it," Louise replied patiently. "The only thing I'm trying to make clear is that Jean and I had nothing to do with the substitution of the ring."

Both the sisters strongly suspected Dotti, and Louise asked, "Mrs. Cracken, did Mr. Dotti and his wife give you any treatments in your stateroom?"

"Yes, they did, but I don't see what that has to do with the disappearance of my ring," the woman replied acidly.

"It might have a great deal to do with it," Louise said quietly, thinking of the time she and Jean had first seen the beautiful ruby and had suspected Mrs. Dotti of listening outside the door.

The Danas regretted that the two hypnotists had left the *Balaska* and could not be searched. The girls hoped that the English detective had trailed them, and when the Danas reported their suspicions to the police, the Dottis could be apprehended.

But right now the sisters must exonerate themselves. Jean turned to Mrs. Cracken. "I'm going to get my uncle and have this settled immediately." She hurried off.

By the time Captain Dana arrived, Mrs. Cracken had calmed down considerably. She even admitted that perhaps she had been hasty in accusing the girls of the theft of her ruby.

"But I'll tell you this," she said. "Until I find out who the real thief is, I'll always have a suspicion in my mind about you two."

Captain Dana's eyes blazed. "Well, ma'am, this is fine gratitude for their having risked their necks to take your jewel case to the purser's office when you should have done it yourself at the beginning of the trip. If I hear that you've mentioned your suspicion of Louise and Jean to a single soul, I declare I'll have you brought into court!"

The girls knew that their uncle would never do any such thing, but it had the desired effect on Mrs. Cracken. She apologized halfheartedly to Louise and Jean, assuring them she would say nothing, and walked off with her jewel box.

Uncle Ned turned to his nieces and gave them a big wink. "Well, you girls got your boat in a whirlpool for a while, didn't you?" he asked.

Then, changing the subject, Captain Dana went on, "Some business has come up which will keep me here most of the day. I won't be able to drive to London with you. I want you girls and Aunt Harriet to go on ahead."

He reached into his pocket and brought out a card. On it was the name of a private limousine service. In one corner was written "Your chauffeur is Alfred Durkin."

"Alfred will be waiting for you near the customs counter," Uncle Ned added, "and will introduce himself. You may as well go along now. I'll meet you at the hotel in London."

Louise hurried to the cabin to tell Aunt Harriet, while Jean went outside to inform Evelyn and Doris of the latest plan. When they went ashore Alfred was waiting for them. He proved to be a most pleasant and helpful individual.

"I'm glad t' meet all o' you ladies," he said, beaming. "I've 'ad the pleasure o' drivin' the captain for many a year."

"We're looking forward to the trip," Aunt Harriet said.

After a customs official had inspected and passed the travelers' baggage, Alfred led them to his limousine. Though he was a careful driver, Doris spent the first half hour in a state of terror because of the left-side-of-the-road driving. She alternately closed her eyes or grasped the armrest next to her whenever a car came toward them. Finally, however, she relaxed and enjoyed the rest of the trip.

"I dare say," said Alfred cheerfully, "that when I come t' your country t' visit, I'll spend 'alf me time 'ollerin' while drivin' your roads. It's all in what a chap gets used t', I guess."

During the sixty-mile trip, his passengers were amused by the man's quaint remarks, mostly about his own countrymen. As they passed through a town, with neat rows of houses and trim little gardens, the chauffeur pointed out a man standing on the corner. The fellow looked very unkempt, and his face and hands were covered with soot.

Alfred grinned. "Blimey! That chap must be down from th' collieries, and 'asn't taken time t' wash off the coal dust!"

Toward noontime the party reached the outskirts of the great city of London. Alfred said he would drive his passengers directly to their hotel. After luncheon he would take them sight-seeing.

Traffic was heavy, and consisted mostly of double-deck buses and very small cars. Many of the men driving the cars were tall.

"Alfred, do tall people have to fold up to get in and out?" Jean asked, grinning.

The man laughed good-naturedly. Presently he pulled up in front of the Savoy Hotel. As a porter took their baggage, Alfred said, "I'll meet you 'ere at 'alf before two."

Promptly at one-thirty the three Danas and their friends met him outside the hotel. For the next two hours Alfred drove the group around the city of London. Louise was particularly impressed with the broad, calm Thames River, and with the stately Houses of Parliament on its bank.

Jean especially admired St. Paul's Cathedral.

once badly bombed. She stood gazing for a long time at the church's immense dome, on top of which was a huge lantern in the shape of a ball and cross.

"It's one o' th' finest churches in th' world," said Alfred.

In Westminster Abbey, the group stood silently near the crypts of many of the famous people who had dictated England's history. They paused reverently at the section in the floor beneath which lay the tomb of Britain's Unknown Warrior.

Later, back in the limousine, Evelyn asked Alfred, "Is Piccadilly really a circus?"

The man laughed heartily. "No, miss. Piccadilly's mostly our club and shopping and entertainment district," Then, half closing his eyes, he added, "O' course, th' way some folks dash around there is like bein' in a three-ring circus!"

"It's the same in our country," Aunt Harriet remarked.

Alfred drove them through the theater section of Piccadilly, then along Downing Street. He paused before Number 10 and removed his cap. "The residence o' th' prime ministers," he said. "Cabinet sessions o' th' government are often 'eld 'ere and important decisions for our country made."

Alfred had planned his tour so that they would reach Buckingham Palace at the time of the Changing of the Guard.

"They look pretty 'andsome, don't you think?" he asked the Americans proudly.

"They certainly do," replied Doris, then declared with a romantic sigh that she had never seen handsomer nor more intriguingly uniformed men.

The soldiers wore black trousers, white-belted red coats, and high headgear of shaggy black fur. They stood extremely straight and marched with exquisite precision. As one group left, another took its place, and the marching continued without a pause.

Jean was busy snapping pictures of the men, back of whom was the high iron fence and the beautiful lawns of Buckingham and, in the distance, the palace itself.

"Oh, 'ave a mind," Alfred exclaimed excitedly, "'ere comes the Queen!"

Through the main gate rolled a car. The visitors were thrilled when it came down the street toward them. They waved and nodded, giving little fast curtsies and the Queen smiled at them graciously.

"Oh, I'm so happy I could burst," said Doris.

"You're lucky, miss," declared Alfred. "Thousands o' visitors come 'ere without ever seein' our Queen. Well, I guess we 'ad better be gettin' back t' th' car and movin' along."

Aunt Harriet, Doris, and Evelyn went ahead with him and stepped into the limousine. Just as

"I must talk to you!" the man cried out.

Louise and Jean were about to follow, a voice behind them cried out:

"Stop!"

The sisters turned to see a man about forty years old running toward them. He was tall and had rather large features and an athletic build.

Rushing up to the sisters, he cried, "You're the Danas. I must talk to you. I'm a detective!"

Astonished, Louise and Jean paused. The stranger went on, "My name is Rankin—Henry Rankin—from New York. I was the detective on the recent trip of the *Balaska*."

"How did you find us?" Louise asked, wanting to be sure that this man was really that person.

"Your uncle told me you'd be sight-seeing and I was certain you'd come here at this time to see the Changing of the Guard," the man explained. "I was sorry I couldn't introduce myself on shipboard, but I had to obey the rules."

Jean asked Mr. Rankin why he wanted to see them.

"Because I've just learned that you girls may be in danger."

Aunt Harriet, who had leaned out of the car to listen, looked disturbed. "Oh, dear! What is this all about?"

Mr. Rankin said that after attending to some business of his own in London, he had stopped at the police department.

"I wanted to find out where the Dottis were

staying, and whether anything suspicious had been discovered about them. I learned that the couple had double-crossed the police! Apparently they suspected they might be followed and threw their trailers off the scent."

"You mean they've vanished?" Jean asked in alarm.

Mr. Rankin nodded. "The story is this: An English detective followed them to a hotel here in London. The Dottis were in a cab and got out with four pieces of luggage, the same as they had had on shipboard. They checked in at the hotel and were taken to a room.

"The detective waited in the lobby a little while, then phoned their room. He was planning to pose as a reporter and get an interview on hypnotic techniques.

"But there was no answer, so he hurried upstairs and knocked on the Dottis' door. When he received no response, he took the manager into his confidence and the door was unlocked. The Dottis' baggage was there, filled with magazines they had bought at the station. It was obvious that they had left the place for good."

"But," Louise put in, "surely they must have had the clothes and other things they'd brought on the trip. What did they carry them away in?"

"The police and I discussed that," said Mr. Rankin. "We feel that the Dottis had bags which fitted tightly inside their suitcases. These were so cleverly put together that the trick was not evident to the customs men. While in the taxi, the couple apparently took out the inside bags which held their possessions."

"But where did they leave them?" Evelyn spoke up. "In the taxi?"

"Exactly," said Mr. Rankin. "It's my guess that they asked the taxi driver to wait for them at a rear exit of the hotel with their personal luggage. After checking in, the Dottis chose a time when nobody was in their corridor, hurried down the stairway, and out the rear of the hotel."

"Very clever," said Aunt Harriet. "But what a strange thing to do!"

"One thing is certain," said Jean flatly. "The Dottis are *not* honest people."

"You're right," said Mr. Rankin. "They're probably the jewel thieves you suspected them of being. This means they won't stop at anything to gain their ends. I believe the Dottis are dangerous. That was why I felt it my duty to warn you about them."

CHAPTER XII

Sight-seeing Detectives

AFTER the detective had given his warning about the hypnotists, he hurried away. As he disappeared from view in St. James Park, the Danas and their friends rode off.

"I'm very much upset to hear about the Dottis' actions," said Aunt Harriet. "You girls *must* watch out for them."

"We will," Louise promised. "But we'll probably never see the Dottis again," she added, trying to assuage her aunt's fears.

"Yes," said Jean. "Enrico may just be an ordinary jewel thief and have nothing whatever to do with the winking ruby mystery."

"I hope that you're right," said Aunt Harriet. "Of course I want you girls to help Gino Marzi, but I don't want you to get involved in any danger while doing it."

When they reached the Savoy Hotel, Uncle Ned was there. He was disturbed to learn the latest news of the two hypnotists.

"If they're really unscrupulous people, let the police locate them. Now, let's forget everything unpleasant. I'm going to take you to Simpson's tonight for some of the finest roast beef this side of the Atlantic."

The meal at the famous restaurant, from appetizer to dessert, proved to be all that Uncle Ned had predicted. When they had finished the last bit of delicious custard pudding with strawberries, the girls groaned, declaring that they had never eaten so much at one time in their lives.

"I didn't know there were such big, juicy helpings of roast beef in the world!" Jean declared.

Captain Dana laughed jovially. "We had to have some kind of celebration, didn't we? I'll be sad when you all leave me tomorrow."

It was at the London airport next morning that he said good-by to them. He wished Aunt Harriet and the girls a good trip to Florence and a successful outcome of the mystery.

"We'll certainly do our best," Louise promised him. "It would be wonderful to help restore Gino's memory."

After they were air-borne, the girls never took their eyes from the scenery below. In the English Channel ocean liners looked like toy boats. When they flew over the French Alps, the high mountains seemed artificial with their green and brown scenery. Luncheon was served and a little later the girls had their first glimpse of the Mediterranean.

"It certainly is blue, just like the books say," Evelyn remarked. "How lovely it is!"

The pilot was not flying so high now and the passengers could get a clear view of the beautiful rocky mountainside of the Riviera. Large villas of various colors, with roofs which glinted in the sunlight, dotted the landscape. Each was surrounded by a profusion of flowers in yellow, pink, and purple. Bougainvillea grew rampant. Lush green vines, shrubbery, and grass looked like a patterned carpet.

Along the shore line were white beaches and large hotels. A broad water-front avenue flanked with palm trees could be seen at times.

"I've never seen a more fascinating place," Doris said enthusiastically. "Now I know why artists love it here."

"I'd say you're losing your own heart," Evelyn gibed.

The plane came down at Nice and the passengers had a chance to walk around the airport for a while. Then they got aboard again and set off for Rome. Circling in over this city of stately buildings and old ruins, the girls caught their breath.

"Look, there's the Colosseum!" exclaimed Jean.

"And that must be the Victor Emmanuel monument—the one they call the 'wedding cake'!" Doris said, pointing to a brilliant white building which stood out from the soft grays and tans of the ancient city. "I wish we could stay here."

"We'll come back," Aunt Harriet promised.

Finally the last part of their journey began. It was late afternoon when they flew into the Florence airport and took a taxi into the city. Driving through the narrow cobblestone streets, the girls gazed in amazement at the ancient stone buildings. They rose straight up from the sidewalks.

"I feel as if I were walking right back into history!" Louise remarked.

"Some of these buildings," Aunt Harriet said, "were the homes of the Medici, the rulers of Florence in the fifteenth century."

All the windows were barred and entrance doors were of heavy iron, or wood with iron trimmings.

"People in those days believed in thorough protection," Louise observed, "the way they barricaded themselves inside."

"They had to," said Aunt Harriet. "Households during those times were in constant danger of attack by raiders or other enemy groups."

Presently the driver pulled up in front of their hotel. It faced a street running along the Arno River. Fortunately, the travelers' two large rooms were in the front of the building, overlooking the water. Not far away was the famous ancient covered bridge, the Ponte Vecchio, which had survived several fierce wars.

"We'll walk across the bridge while we're here," said Aunt Harriet. "You'll want to buy some things in the shops there."

After dinner the Danas and their friends strolled along the Arno. The visitors found themselves walking side by side not only with natives of Florence, but with tourists of various nationalities.

"Isn't this exciting?" Doris observed. "Do you know that within just one block I heard six different languages being spoken?"

Groups of young people, singing gay Italian folk songs, ambled along the narrow sidewalk. The only disturbing note in the tranquil scene was an occasional motorcycle which roared past.

Evelyn remarked dreamily, "The old, slow romantic life mixed with our modern age of speed. I adore it!"

Long after the travelers had gone to bed, they lay awake, musing on the truth of Evelyn's comment. From the street the music of old Italian ballads and snatches of operatic arias drifted up.

As the sweet melodies died away the Danas' thoughts turned to their mystery—the sadness of Gino Marzi's condition, the unscrupulous Dottis, the mysterious Carlo. Louise and Jean wondered, as they finally became drowsy, what lay ahead of them in trying to solve the mystery.

"Tomorrow we ought to pick up a good clue

about where the Marzi family is," said Louise, yawning broadly.

In the morning a Continental breakfast of hot rolls and sweet buns with milk and coffee was served in their rooms. Directly afterward, everyone dressed. The Danas wore light-colored cottons. Louise's was a sunbacked style with a bolero and the others declared she could pass for a Florentine.

"Here's the Marzis' address," Louise said, checking it in her purse. "Let's go!"

They went downstairs to the lobby. There they found a smiling, curly-haired, young man waiting for them. They learned that Uncle Ned had made arrangements for him to act as guide and interpreter.

"This is a great honor," the young man said. "I have been interpreter for many people but never for lady detectives. My name is Dominick."

The girls laughed and Louise said, "We've solved a few mysteries in foreign countries but the language has always been a barrier. This time we won't have to worry with you acting as our interpreter."

This remark pleased Dominick, who was eager to start at once in his new role. He led them outside where a tiny car stood at the curb. They all squeezed in. Louise showed Dominick the Marzi address, then the driver started off.

The ride proved to be an unforgettable experience. Dominick kept his hand on the horn almost constantly, causing the people in the crowded streets to scatter out of his way. Then, with a yank of the brake, he stopped abruptly at a narrow three-story stone house. Like most of the others, its windows were barred.

Dominick jumped from the car and rapped on the front door. There was no response.

"Nobody's here," he told the others.

"Let's speak to some of the Marzis' neighbors," Louise suggested.

She and Jean alighted and walked with Dominick to the house on the right. A buxom woman came to the door. In reply to Dominick's question she said that she had no idea where the Marzis had gone. The searchers tried three other residences. The answer was the same.

"I guess we give up." Dominick shrugged.

"Oh, no," said Jean firmly. "We've just begun."

"I see." Dominick chuckled. "American girl detectives, they have own way of working."

"We'll try a few more houses," said Louise, heading for one a short distance up the street.

A beautiful girl about eighteen years old opened the door. She too told Dominick that she did not know where Mrs. Marzi and her daughter Angela had gone.

"Ask her," suggested Louise, "if she can tell us the name of any of the Marzis' relatives or friends."

Dominick translated the question. The young woman's dark eyes danced. She spoke for nearly a minute, then Dominick interpreted.

"She says Angela had a sweetheart. He may know where the Marzis are. The man is Tony Moreno. He plays the violin in a restaurant."

"Oh, that's wonderful! Louise cried. "Thank her very much."

At this Jean giggled. "I can do that myself." Turning to the young woman, she said, "*Grazie!*"

The Italian girl looked pleased. "*Prego*," she replied.

"She says 'You are welcome,' " Dominick translated.

As he and the girls walked back to the car he told them that the restaurant where Tony Moreno played was on the other side of the Ponte Vecchio. "It's called the Ristorante Arno Giardino."

"Let's have luncheon there and speak to him," Louise proposed.

"That is fine," said Dominick. "Meantime, I will show you some of our beautiful churches and art galleries."

For the next two hours Aunt Harriet and the girls saw paintings by such famous old Italian masters as Leonardo da Vinci and Botticelli. They gazed in awe at the magnificent churches built many centuries before.

Jean, who had been silent for some time, finally spoke up, her eyes twinkling. "When all this was being done, our country was still in the hands of the Indians!"

At twelve o'clock the girls noticed that shops were closing and blinds being pulled down. They mentioned this to Dominick.

He smiled and explained that all business ceased from about twelve to three. "It is not like what I hear is your way in America. Here we take a long rest from twelve to three. But our people do not go home at five o'clock from the offices and shops like you do. They work until seven."

"When do people eat at night?" Doris asked him curiously.

"Oh, nine o'clock maybe. We have four meals each day instead of three, as in your country. We have something to eat, little cakes maybe, about five or six o'clock."

Dominick parked his car near the Ponte Vecchio and the group walked across the old bridge. They made several small purchases. All felt that Aunt Harriet had picked the prize—a dainty handkerchief bordered with exquisite Italian handmade lace.

"What did you buy?" she asked Jean.

"A blouse for Applecore. It's embroidered in every color of the rainbow." She held it up.

"Poor Applecore," Louise teased, "do you want her to look like a gypsy?"

As they reached the far end of the bridge, Dominick said the restaurant was not far away. It proved to be a delightful place facing the water. The charming one-story building was set in a large garden. All the flowers were in full bloom.

Dominick secured a table on a porch overlooking the river. From this point they could also see the five-piece orchestra in the garden. There was one violinist.

"That's Tony Moreno," Dominick told them.

"Would it be all right," Louise asked, "to send a note to Tony and ask him to come to our table whenever he can?"

"Yes, indeed," said Dominick. "I'll write one."

He picked up a menu card and wrote a message on the back of it, then requested the waiter to take the card to the violinist. The others watched as it was delivered and saw Tony nod his head.

"He'll see us. Good!" said Louise.

As the visitors were finishing their delicious desert of Italian pastry, Tony came to the table and sat down in the extra chair. Apparently recognizing that Aunt Harriet and the girls were Americans, he said in English, "You send for me?"

"Yes," replied Louise, smiling at the violinist. "I believe you know Gino Marzi."

A look of amazement came into Tony's eyes. "Yes, I do. He send me message?"

"Not exactly," Louise replied.

She told him of Gino's present misfortune and that Captain Dana was very eager to get in touch with the man's family. "Can you tell us where Mrs. Marzi and Angela are?"

Tony lowered his eyes as a sad expression crept over his face. Finally he raised his head.

"My Angela, she leave me without a word. I am scare something dreadful has happen to her."

"Oh, I'm so sorry," said Louise quickly. "Then you have no idea where she is?"

Tony shook his head despairingly. "I only know a little about Angela's family, so I cannot say how to find anybody. I met Gino one time but never the other brother."

"Gino has a brother?" Jean asked with interest.

"Yes," Tony answered. "One time Angela tell me she have brother by name of Carlo."

"Carlo!" the Dana sisters chorused.

"You not know about him?" the violinist asked in surprise.

"No, we didn't," Louise replied. "Where is Carlo?"

"I do not know," Tony said. "Mrs. Marzi and Angela, they never talk again about him."

"Have you any idea why?" Jean asked him.

"No." Tony said he had assumed that Carlo lived permanently in some foreign country and his family never saw him.

"Do you have an idea that he might be in trouble?" Louise questioned.

Tony could not answer this. But he eagerly offered to help in any way he could to solve the mystery.

"I love Angela," he said. The violinist smiled pleadingly at the Danas. "You bring back my Angela to me and I love you too! Tell you what, I got key to Marzi house. Sometime I used to leave groceries in kitchen for them. Maybe you go there with me and you—what you say—like to do a police snoop?"

Tony's quaint remark made the others laugh. "That's great," said Jean. "We'll go to the house and try to pick up a clue as to where the Marzis went."

She asked when Tony might have some free time to accompany them. He asked where they were staying, and when Jean told him the name of their hotel, he said:

"I will come there five o'clock—*esattamente!* We go on big search for my Angela."

CHAPTER XIII

A Delaying Upset

IT SEEMED to the anxious Americans that five o'clock would never arrive. Dominick had left them and they wandered around the streets for an hour.

Evelyn suddenly chuckled. "Louise," she said, "you're going to hypnotize your wrist watch if you keep staring at it!"

"All right," said Louise, grinning. "I suggest that we fill in the time by taking this sight-seeing bus. It goes to the Medici palaces." She indicated a bus on the street corner.

They climbed in, paid their fare to the English-speaking driver guide, and sat down. A moment later a plump, breathless woman got in and sat down heavily in a front seat.

"Driver," she said, with a broad American accent, "will you please tell me where Firenze is?"

The man, startled and amused, said, "You're sitting in it, Madam."

To the Danas' utter amazement, the woman arose and looked at the seat! As the girls tried hard to refrain from laughing, the guide patiently explained that Firenze was the Italian name for Florence.

The trip to the palace fascinated Aunt Harriet and her group. They marveled at the huge ancient tapestries on the walls with their intricate pictures. The tapestries looked as if they had recently been woven, instead of centuries ago.

When the trip was over, Doris remarked, "I have a feeling that from now on we'll be so busy solving the mystery, we won't have any time to shop. I'd like to stop sight-seeing for a while and buy a set of dishes I saw and send it to my family."

"A good idea," Aunt Harriet agreed. "We'll all shop." The group separated, with each of the girls planning to buy an article which had interested her most.

Doris's dishes were decorated with the graceful Italian lily. Louise and Evelyn purchased delicate figurines, while Jean bought an old religious painting on a wood background. When the group met at the hotel, Aunt Harriet had an armful of beautiful cutwork linen.

As they admired one another's purchases, Evelyn declared, laughing, "I couldn't buy any more souvenirs if I wanted to. I've spent all my money!"

The others admitted that they too were in the same predicament. Shopping in Florence had proved entirely too tempting!

After they had freshened up a bit, they met Tony Moreno in the lobby. Since it was not a long walk to the house where the Marzis had lived, they decided to go there on foot.

The Danas and their friends, looking in every shopwindow they passed, were not aware they had reached the Marzis' street. Suddenly Tony cried out:

"Look! A man and a woman! They just come from Angela's house!"

The Danas looked up and gasped. *The couple were Enrico and Lena Dotti!*

At this moment Lena turned around and caught sight of the Danas. A look of fright crossed her face. She grabbed her husband's arm, said something to him, and the two began to run down the street.

Louise and Jean immediately dashed after them, the other girls following. The chase led around corners, through alleyways, and across the public market. For seconds the Danas would lose sight of the Dottis, then see them again. Soon Louise and Jean had far outdistanced their friends and were gaining on the pair.

"There they go into that leather-goods shop!" Jean called out.

To the amazement of the owner and his assistant, the hypnotists and their pursuers rushed through the front door, out the back, across a garden and into the rear of another shop.

The Dottis sped through it and went out the street door. Louise and Jean were forced to slow down to avoid several customers who were entering the shop at the moment. By the time they reached the street, the hypnotist and his wife were out of sight.

"Now which way do we go?" Jean asked, panting.

An American woman bystander, evidently guessing that the girls were looking for the couple, pointed to the left. Once more the girls started off. Not seeing the Dottis ahead of them, Louise and Jean assumed that they had turned the next corner. They put on more speed and reached the intersection in a few seconds.

"Look out!" a girl called, but the warning came too late.

A man wheeling a flower cart had reached the corner at the same instant the Danas had. Jean, in the lead, ran full tilt into the cart, knocking it over. The containers of bright-colored flowers scattered in every direction. Jean herself sprawled headlong onto the sidewalk.

"*Cristoforo Colombo!*" the flower vendor cried out, slapping his forehead with one hand.

Louise helped Jean to her feet. "Are you hurt?"

she asked. When Jean shook her head, Louise turned to the man. "We're so sorry."

The man surveyed the wreckage mournfully. "*Multo triste!*" He heaved a great sigh.

"Yes, it is sad," said Louise. She gathered that the man could not speak English.

There was only one way to make up for the accident. She opened her purse, took out a five-dollar bill, and handed it to the vendor.

The man smiled. "*Buone signorine.*"

The Danas did not feel much like "Good ladies," however. Jean's mishap had caused them to lose track of the Dottis completely!

"We may as well go back to the Marzi home," Jean sighed. "At least, we may be able to find out what the Dottis were doing there."

"What puzzles me is how they got into the place," said Louise. "Could they have had a key? If so, from whom did they get it?"

The girls started to retrace their steps, but soon realized that they were lost. Fortunately, Louise still had the paper on which Uncle Ned had written the Marzis' address.

"I'll show this to a policeman," she said.

At the corner an English-speaking officer gave them directions. When they reached the house, the Danas found that only Tony was there. He said he had remained on guard in case any other troublesome person should appear. A few moments later Aunt Harriet, Doris, and Evelyn appeared.

"Did you find the Dottis?" Evelyn asked eagerly.

"No," Louise replied. "But I'd like to take up the search later."

"Now we go inside?" Tony asked. When Louise nodded, he took the key from his pocket and opened the heavy door.

He stood aside as Aunt Harriet, then the girls, entered, gallantly handing each one a small flashlight he carried in his coat. "I get these special for you," Tony said. "I hear detectives carry lights always. This house, it is never bright inside."

As the searchers swept their beams over the dim, heavily curtained rooms, a dismaying sight met their eyes. The place was a shambles!

Tony cried out something in Italian which the girls could not understand. Then in English he added, "My Angela's home! And her good mother's! This is wickedness!"

As the group made a closer study of the hall, living room, and dining room, they saw that several beautiful old chests had been broken open, apparently in a search for something valuable.

"Do you suppose the winking ruby could have been hidden here?" Jean whispered to Louise.

"It's a good guess," her sister conceded. "Maybe the Dottis thought so too. Let's hope they didn't find it! I think we should notify the local police of our suspicions about them."

Jean nodded and Louise took a note pad and pencil from her purse. She wrote the message, then asked Tony to take it to headquarters. He nodded and hurried off.

The others now began an investigation of the house for some clue to the Marzis' whereabouts and also for the ruby. Jean went through to the kitchen. A few minutes later she called out:

"Come to the kitchen, everybody! See what I've found—" The girl's words seemed to be choked off.

Miss Dana and the girls hurried to the rear of the house. To their amazement, Jean was not in sight.

"Oh, something dreadful must have happened to her!" Aunt Harriet cried out.

CHAPTER XIV

An Ancient Trap

For a few moments the group stared in stupefaction about the disordered kitchen. The doors of an old-fashioned cupboard yawned open, but there was nothing inside. A door to an empty pantry stood wide open. Jean was not there.

"It's ghostly!" said Doris, trembling a little. At the top of her voice she cried out, "Jean! Jean! Where are you?"

There was no answer. The house seemed ominously silent.

Louise was the first one to take a practical view of the matter. "Jean is here somewhere and we're going to find her!" she said determinedly. "Suppose we divide forces. Aunt Harriet, will you and Doris go upstairs and look around? Evelyn and I can search down here."

Miss Dana and Doris, beaming their flashlights ahead of them, started up the back stairway.

Louise, noticing a rear entrance to the kitchen, said, "There's probably a garden beyond. Let's look in it, Evelyn."

The door was stuck but finally they opened it and looked into the garden. It was overgrown and untidy, although flowers bloomed in profusion around an artistic well house. Jean was not there.

"She must be upstairs then." Evelyn sighed. "Let's go help your aunt and Doris search."

They, too, went to the rooms above and every inch of the place was searched. Still there was no sign of the missing girl.

Thoroughly frightened by this time, the group was wondering what to do next, when they heard pounding on the front door.

"It must be Tony," said Louise, and hurried down the front stairway to open the door.

Tony stood there with a policeman. "I bring you *carabiniere*," he stated. "He want to look over house."

"He can help us with something even more important right now," said Louise, and told him of Jean's disappearance.

The policeman looked worried, but Tony seemed unconcerned. "Maybe your sister is behind secret wall," he suggested.

"Secret wall?" Louise repeated. "Where is that?"

"In the kitchen. I will show you," Tony offered. "In old Italian home sometime they make hiding place from foreign soldiers or robbers."

He led the way there and pointed to one wall. Alongside the open cupboard was a long wooden panel.

"Angela tell me about this. I will try to open."

Tony looked at one end of the panel carefully. Then, finding a lock, he released it and began easing the door open. Beyond, the others could see a deep closet with a series of stone shelves at the back. On them stood several ancient crocks.

"Why, this—" Louise began, then stared disbelievingly.

In the floor was a circular pit. Wedged down into it was Jean Dana! Only her head could be seen and there was a gag across her mouth!

"Jean!" Louise cried, dashing forward to her sister.

Quickly Tony and the *carabiniere* pulled the imprisoned girl out, and Louise tore off the gag.

"Th-thanks," Jean said, leaning heavily on Tony.

As he helped the bedraggled girl to a chair, Aunt Harriet bent over her niece solicitously.

"Are you all right, dear? What happened?"

It took Jean a few moments to compose herself. Then she said, "I'm all right. But I sure had a scare. I thought nobody was ever going to find me!"

Jean related that just before she called to the others to come to the kitchen, she had discovered

Louise quickly tore off the gag.

the secret panel. As she turned to pick up her flashlight, Jean said, someone had grabbed her from behind, stuffed a handkerchief into her mouth, dragged her inside the closet and closed the panel.

"I couldn't see anything," Jean went on. "The man held my arms to my sides and lowered me into the narrow pit. I guess it's a dried-up well. My hands were wedged so tightly against me that I couldn't move them to reach up and pull myself out. Later, he tied another handkerchief across the gag."

"Where's the man?" Louise asked.

Jean told her that he had stayed in the hiding place for some time. The two of them could hear everything that the others in the kitchen said.

"When he knew that everyone had left the first floor," Jean went on, "he slid the door open, closed it again, and apparently left the house."

"He must have been with the Dottis," Louise surmised. "When we showed up so suddenly, he must have hidden in the secret closet."

"Yes," her sister agreed. "And probably he hoped to pick up some information from us."

Suddenly the policeman smiled. In English he said, "You are fine detectives."

Jean smiled ruefully. "I wonder if we really are. Detectives don't get caught as easily as I did."

"Oh, yes, they do," the officer answered. "I got caught myself once!"

Louise asked Jean to describe her captor.

"I can't tell you much, for I never saw his face. But he was extremely thin and breathed in short, nervous gasps."

"I will report this to my captain," said the *carabiniere*. "First I will investigate here for clues."

He walked through the entire house, making notes. Then he went off. In the meantime, Jean had tried to get water from a faucet in order to wash her face and hands, but the supply was turned off. Tony went out to a well in the garden and soaked his handkerchief. He brought it into the house and handed it to Jean.

"My Angela, she never want to have dirt on face or hands, either. Maybe you would like to use this."

Jean smiled. "You're a lifesaver, Tony."

After she had wiped the ancient dust of the closet from her face, hands, and neck, Tony miraculously produced a tiny whisk broom from his coat pocket. He brushed her dress.

"Now you are good-as-new detective," he said.

"Let's join the others," Jean suggested.

All this time Aunt Harriet and the other girls had been searching the house for a secret compartment which might hold the winking ruby. As Jean and Tony left the kitchen, she asked the violinist if the Marzi family had ever owned a valuable ruby.

"I never hear of one," the young man replied,

then he added shyly, "My Angela and I, we talk most about our love. We always say we get married soon."

Jean wondered whether Angela knew about the winking ruby. And if she did, whether it was a secret in the Marzi family which she did not want to reveal.

"Any luck?" Jean asked, as she and Tony entered the living room.

They saw Evelyn poking among some charred papers in the old fireplace grate. Suddenly the girl picked up part of a burned letter and began to read it.

"This may be a clue!" she cried out excitedly.

CHAPTER XV

The Unexpected Reunion

"THIS burned letter is written in Italian," said Evelyn, handing it to Tony.

The young violinist turned his flashlight on the charred paper and began to read. At first there was amazement on his face, then finally a broad smile broke out.

"This letter is from my Angela!" he exclaimed excitedly. "She write me that she and her mother are hide out in Ascona, Switzerland!"

"How wonderful!" Louise exclaimed. "Now we can find them."

"But why didn't Angela mail the letter?" Evelyn asked, puzzled.

Tony could not answer this and his smile faded. Doris suggested that possibly someone else had made it impossible for Angela to send the message. She might have hidden the note temporarily in the fireplace, then had been forced to leave before she could retrieve it.

Jean shook her head. "That doesn't explain why Angela never wrote to Tony from Ascona," she said. "It's my guess that the Marzis had been threatened and Angela felt it best not to involve Tony."

Hearing this, the young man stood up very straight. "I love Angela. Nobody can stop me from seeing her." He looked intently at the Americans. "Will you go with me to Ascona and help to find my Angela?"

"I'd like to," said Jean. She turned to Aunt Harriet. "Do you think it would be possible?"

Miss Dana smiled. "I'm sure that's what your Uncle Ned would want. You detectives have an assignment to find the Marzis."

The violinist said he would ask the owner of the restaurant where he worked if he might have a few days' leave. "I will telephone you later," he said. "And now I must get back to my job."

Tony locked the house and said good-by to the Americans. Then he hurried off and they walked slowly back to their hotel.

"Evelyn, you should receive a medal for finding that clue," said Louise.

Evelyn grinned. "I'll settle for a free supper."

An hour later Tony telephoned to say he had secured the leave. He would rent a car and call for them the following morning at nine o'clock.

As the girls packed, Doris remarked, "I suppose Tony will be in such a hurry to get to Ascona he won't let us stop to do any sight-seeing. But I just hate missing so many wonderful things."

Aunt Harriet smiled wisely. "Leave it to me," she said with a wink. "I'll need some rest now and then. You know my back can't stand long rides."

The girls giggled and knew that Miss Dana would arrange matters so they would see the main points of interest on the trip.

The first stretch of the trip was as far as Bologna. Here the travelers walked around the broad streets and saw the famous old university. After eating, they continued their journey until they came to Milan.

"We will stay overnight here," Aunt Harriet announced. "We've done enough riding for one day."

Tony looked a little annoyed, but Miss Dana had her way. She even insisted that before leaving the next morning, the girls should visit the great Cathedral of Milan with its fine Gothic architecture. Then they hurried off to view Leonardo da Vinci's painting of "The Last Supper" at the small church of Santa Maria delle Grazie.

"It has had to be restored several times," the guide told them. "The dampness of the wall on which the fresco is painted is causing great damage."

The travelers looked at it reverently, then it

was time to meet Tony. He had been patient all this time, but now he urged that they start for Ascona.

"Please," he said pleadingly, "I want to see my Angela today."

"We'll go right away," Aunt Harriet promised.

As they drove along, the countryside became less populated and the road wound through pleasant farm areas. At one point they saw a man working on a hillside. It was so steep that in order to keep his balance while working, he had staked himself to the ground!

"That's farming the hard way," Jean remarked, laughing.

Tony smiled. "In Italy sometimes we must work the hardest way outdoor. But it is the healthy way. And we use all ground we can."

The group lunched at a hotel on beautiful Lake Como, then set off once more. Presently they came to the border of Switzerland, where their luggage was once more inspected and quickly passed by customs.

Tony drove on. After a while he said, "Now we climb and climb."

How true his words were! The mountains grew higher and were so beautiful that the travelers ohed and ahed at every turn of the road. Finally they reached Ascona, nestled among the verdant mountains on Lake Maggiore.

"I hope my Angela is happy here," Tony said, sighing.

He told the group that Italian was the language usually spoken in this part of Switzerland and that he would act as their interpreter. They questioned shopkeepers and residents about the Marzis, but no one had heard of them. The violinist became more and more discouraged.

"I'm sure that we'll find them," said Louise kindly. "One place we haven't tried yet is a bakery. Sooner or later everyone goes to a bakery."

Tony took heart. The searchers hurried along the main street and presently came to a shop with an intriguing window display of twisted loaves of bread and appetizing pastries. Tony went inside. He was gone only a couple of minutes. Then he returned, smiling excitedly.

"My Angela is not far away!" he said. "We go down, then up, then down again. We find her at the end."

The others were amused at the directions, but followed the young man. In his eagerness he was almost running. Doris started to hurry after him, but Miss Dana held her back.

"How about letting Tony and Angela have a few minutes alone?" she suggested.

"Yes, we should," Doris agreed.

They kept the young man in sight, but stopped some distance from the tiny Swiss chalet which he entered. Ten minutes later they approached the house and knocked.

Tony himself opened the door. His arm was around a beautiful girl of eighteen. She had brown flashing eyes, even white teeth, and dark, wavy hair. Both were smiling ecstatically.

"See, is she not an angel, I ask you?" the young man said.

Tony introduced his fiancée, who in turn invited the visitors to come in. They walked into the living room, where a rather stout, blond woman sat on a straight-back chair.

"My mother, Frau Marzi," Angela said. "Mother was born in Germany and likes to be called Frau Marzi."

The woman greeted her callers pleasantly and asked them to be seated. She said she was amazed to learn from Tony that the Americans had come from such a great distance to find her and Angela.

Louise turned to Tony. "You haven't told Frau Marzi and Angela why we wanted to see them?"

"No," the violinist answered. "We are so happy to be together again. There is no time."

Frau Marzi leaned forward in her chair. "You bring some news, perhaps?"

Louise nodded. Much as she disliked doing so, Louise told of Gino Marzi's collapse and the fact that he was suffering from amnesia.

"He is not well enough to travel, or my uncle would have brought him to Italy."

Frau Marzi had risen from her chair. Now she looked out of the window and the girls could see a tear trickle down one cheek.

Louise went over and spoke quietly to her. "At least one part of the mystery is cleared up. We've found you and that should make your son feel better. If the whole mystery can only be solved, I'm sure it will restore Gino to full health."

"There is more mystery?" Frau Marzi asked, puzzled.

Louise told her of the strange message which the violinist had given to Captain Dana. "Please tell us about Carlo and about the winking ruby," the young detective begged. "We want to help you all we can."

Mrs. Marzi looked at Angela, then both looked at Tony. Finally Angela said, "Mama, I think we should tell these kind people our secret. We kept it so long. Now we have no money and Carlo has not come back."

"All right, my dear," her mother conceded. "You speak English better than I do. You tell about our troubles."

Angela began an amazing story. She said that Carlo was Gino's twin brother. About three years ago he had gone to Germany to hunt for a priceless gem called the winking ruby. Angela paused and hung her head.

"We did not hear from Carlo for a long time. Then an Italian friend of his, named Sal Riccio, came one day and told us that Carlo was in hiding. He said my brother had stolen a large sum of money. After he had spent all of it, he hid in the mountain."

Angela went on to say that Carlo's conscience had begun to bother him and he had resolved to pay back all the money. Afraid to come out in the open, he had decided to stay in hiding while doing this.

"He asked us for the money. We were to pay it to him in small amounts."

As she paused, Jean said, "And you sent the money?"

Angela nodded. "Sal Riccio used to come every once in a while and take it with him."

"Are you sure that this Sal Riccio is honest?" Jean spoke up. "Did you have any way of knowing that Carlo had sent him?"

"Oh, yes," Angela replied. "Carlo sent a letter to us which Sal delivered."

Tony now asked why she and her mother had fled from Florence. Angela looked as if she were about to cry, but she answered:

"For two years we were sending the money which Gino mailed home to us. Mama and I added what we could spare of our own. But finally we had only enough left to live on."

Aunt Harriet asked if Gino Marzi knew about this.

Angela replied, "We did not tell Gino we had

given away all his money until the last time he was home. Gino became very angry and said he was going to see this Sal Riccio."

"Where does Riccio live?" Jean queried.

"In Firenze," Angela replied. "But he makes trips to Germany very often."

Louise asked what happened when Gino talked with him.

"Sal Riccio was not at home," Angela said, "and Gino had to leave, for the *Balaska* was sailing. Gino told us to hide and not pay any more money. He would try to go to Germany soon and find Carlo. Gino did not believe the story."

Tony looked at Angela, a hurt expression on his face. "Why you not tell your Tony this? I help you."

Frau Marzi answered the question. "You are a fine man, Tony. If our Carlo is a thief, Gino and I cannot let Angela marry you."

"That make no difference," said Tony stanchly. "And no need to make Angela burn the letter to me."

"We are proud people," said Frau Marzi. "The mystery about Carlo must be solved before we can have a wedding."

The visitors looked at one another in dismay. Now they were confronted with a new problem. Should the Dana girls find Carlo and prove him to be a thief, the romance between Angela and Tony, according to Italian family custom, would be over.

"Don't give up hope," Aunt Harriet said to the Marzis and Tony. "Carlo must be a fine character like you and some day everything will be straightened out."

All this time Louise and Jean had been thinking about the unscrupulous people they suspected of being connected with the mystery. Should they add Sal Riccio to the list? Louise asked Angela what the man looked like, and learned he was extremely thin and breathed in short, nervous gasps.

"Why, he's the one who imprisoned me!" said Jean. "And right in your own house, too!"

The Marzis were thunderstruck when Jean related her experience of being imprisoned in the secret closet.

"Now I know the story about my brother is not true!" Angela cried out. "Riccio is a wicked man!"

"And the note he brought," said Louise, "probably was a forgery."

Frau Marzi said she hoped this was true. She had tried hard not to believe that her son was a thief. "But why did he never write to us from Germany?" Suddenly a frightening thought came to her. "Do you think our Carlo could be a prisoner of these wicked people?"

"I think it's very possible," Louise replied. "And I understand from Tony that Carlo is an expert at making jewelry and artificial gems. My sister and I think some jewel thieves carry inexpensive rings with them that look like very valuable ones. These people follow the owners of costly rings, and when they get a chance, they cleverly make a substitution. We believe this happened on the *Balaska*."

"That is bad," said Frau Marzi. "Please go on with your story."

Jean took it up. "We suspect that these same jewel thieves are looking for the winking ruby. Maybe they met your son in Germany and they are forcing him to make jewelry for them."

"What dreadful people!" Angela exclaimed.

Louise nodded. "I even think they're pretending to Carlo that they're selling the pieces he makes. They may give him some of the money which you have been sending and tell him it is what they get for his jewelry."

Evelyn had a supposition too. She thought that Sal Riccio probably had taken Carlo's house key from him and used it to let himself and the Dottis into the Marzis' house.

"They probably were looking for the winking ruby."

"But it is not there, of course," Angela spoke up.

Louise asked why Carlo had gone to Germany to search for the winking ruby. Before answering, Frau Marzi sat up proudly in her chair and smiled.

"I have never told anyone this secret. It has remained in my family. But you Americans and Tony have been so kind, I will tell you."

Frau Marzi went on to say that she had been a member of the Kronen family in Germany. The ancestral home was a castle some miles from Frankfurt.

"It is a ruin now," she said. "Overgrown and abandoned. We just manage to pay the taxes."

After a pause, Frau Marzi said that three hundred years before, her ancestor, the Baroness Kathryn von Kronen, lived there.

"She owned the fabulous ruby. When the castle was under attack by a baron from a neighboring place, she had the gem hidden. The enemy was driven off, but not before they had ruined the castle. The baroness was killed and the hiding place of the winking ruby became a mystery."

"What an interesting story!" said Doris.

"Yes," said Frau Marzi. "If we could find the winking ruby, it would mean so much to me and my family. That was why Carlo went to Germany."

"But you don't know whether he ever reached the castle?" Louise asked her.

Sadly the woman shook her head. Rising from her chair, she walked to a chest of drawers in the room. Opening the top drawer, she drew out a photograph.

"This is Carlo," she said.

The Danas noticed the young man's strong resemblance to Angela. Should the girls ever see Carlo, it would be very easy to identify him.

Suddenly Frau Marzi put her arms around the two Dana sisters. Looking first at one, then the other, she said pleadingly:

"You will go to Germany and save my Carlo?"

CHAPTER XVI

A Missing Passport

"We certainly want to solve this mystery," Louise told Mrs. Marzi, "but a trip to Germany would cost a lot of money."

Jean, less practical, turned to her Aunt Harriet. "We'll just have to find money somehow. I feel sure that Carlo is a prisoner, and we must try to free him!"

Aunt Harriet was thoughtful. "Of course this whole matter could be turned over to the police," she said.

At this remark Mrs. Marzi looked frightened. "Oh, please, let us not do that! My Carlo is innocent of any wrongdoing, I am sure. But these dreadful people who have him in their clutches, they may make it appear as if he is one of them. No, no, we must not tell the police. We must save Carlo first and find out what is going on."

140

Evelyn reminded the others that Gino's message had been, "Save Carlo." She said that perhaps the violinist had figured out the situation, just as his mother had.

"I suppose you're right," Aunt Harriet conceded. "Well, we'll telephone Uncle Ned and see what he can do."

It was decided that the group would spend the night in Ascona and make arrangements for the rest of their trip. Tony and Angela took the Americans to a charming hotel built into the side of the mountain, then the happy couple left them.

"We may as well get started on our plans," said Jean impatiently. "I think we ought to telephone the police in Florence and tell them about Sal Riccio."

"And perhaps they've arrested the Dottis," Louise suggested.

"Oh, I hope so!" said Doris. "Those dreadful people! Why, they may be responsible for breaking up Tony and Angela's marriage!"

"But we'll change that!" Evelyn declared.

The police chief, to whom Louise spoke in Florence, said that so far the hypnotists had eluded the police. It was thought that they were traveling under an assumed name and had left the country.

"We have notified the police in other places to watch for them," the officer said. "And we'll take Riccio into custody for questioning at once."

The Danas' next phone call was trans-Atlantic

to the *Balaska*. It took several hours before contact was made. Uncle Ned was amazed to hear the latest developments.

"You're certainly making progress. My congratulations! And you definitely must go to Germany. But what about Doris and Evelyn?"

"Please contact Doris's parents and Evelyn's brother to see if they'll send more money," Louise requested. "Oh, I'm sure they will when they know how important our errand is."

Uncle Ned promised to get in touch with the Harlands and Franklin Starr. "And don't you worry, my hearties," the captain added. "Their folks will want them to see the job through." He chuckled. "I knew you wouldn't fail me."

"And we've had a wonderful time doing it, too," said Louise gaily.

The group had breakfast the following morning on a terrace overlooking one of the most beautiful countrysides they had seen yet on the trip. Presently the waiter handed Aunt Harriet a cablegram. The girls leaned forward eagerly to hear the contents. It read:

SAIL ON TO VICTORY. AMMUNITION ENCLOSED.

The girls laughed at Uncle Ned's quaint way of giving them permission and sending the money, then gave a whoop of joy. Louise, who had come downstairs early to check on flight schedules, now said:

"We'll have to go back to Milan for a plane to Frankfurt."

Aunt Harriet suggested that it might be advisable to have as few people as possible know where they were going.

"Yes," Louise agreed. "Let's have Tony make our plane reservations for us."

This was agreed upon, and as soon as the young man arrived, they told him of their plans. He was overjoyed to hear that they would continue their sleuthing. After paying their hotel bill, the Americans drove off with him.

Down in the town, Tony stopped at a secluded telephone and made the call to the Milan airport. He returned to the car, smiling, saying that five reservations for a plane the next morning were being held. They must be picked up that evening, however.

"My car, it better behave and get us there," the young man remarked.

The automobile purred along and by late afternoon the travelers reached Milan. Tony drove directly to the airport and Aunt Harriet picked up the tickets. Then Tony drove them to a hotel. As their luggage was being carried inside by porters, the violinist suddenly hugged and kissed each of the travelers.

"I am so happy a man," he said. "You have restored my sweetheart to me!" But the next moment his eyes clouded with worry. "Please try hard to find Carlo. Then everybody be happy all the time."

"You bet we will," said Jean. "And we'll let you know the minute the mystery is solved."

Tony drove off, waving to them. Louise sent her uncle a cablegram telling of their plans, then the travelers ate supper. They had a good night's rest and were up early.

Opening the shutters at her window, Louise gazed across the street. She could look into an office building and was amazed to see that people were already at work. Louise glanced at her watch.

"Why, it's only seven o'clock," she told herself. Then the girl remembered that in this part of the world people worked early in the day and late in the afternoon but not during the middle of the day.

Soon Aunt Harriet and the other girls arose. Directly after breakfast they left the hotel. At the airport a little later they were requested to go to a certain counter and show their passports. In turn, Aunt Harriet, her nieces and Evelyn produced theirs from their handbags.

Doris fumbled for hers. Suddenly a strange, worried look came over her face. "It's gone!" she said. "I can't find it! I've lost my passport!"

The girl's friends turned to her in dismay. "Let me look in your bag," Evelyn requested.

But though Evelyn examined each item carefully, she did not find Doris's passport.

Tears welled up in the unfortunate girl's eyes. "What will I do?" she wailed. "I can't stay here without you!"

"The first thing to do," said Louise, "is to think hard. Maybe you didn't lose the passport out of your bag. Do you recall putting it some place else for safety?"

Doris thought hard. Finally she said, "I seem to remember putting it in one of my suitcases."

The travelers' bags had not yet been put aboard and Doris's two suitcases were retrieved. Quickly the four girls searched them carefully. There was no sign of the passport.

At this point tears rolled down Doris's cheeks. "Y-you'll have to go without me!"

All the girls but Jean had given up the search. She was now pulling everything out of the plastic bags into which Doris had stuffed shoes and other articles. Suddenly she cried out:

"I've found it! Doris, what in the world made you tuck your passport inside a shoe?"

Doris blinked unbelievingly through her tears. Then she smiled sheepishly and gave Jean a hug. "I don't even remember doing such a silly thing."

The passport was taken to the counter, then the travelers were allowed to go through the gate to the waiting plane.

The flight to Frankfurt fascinated the Americans. It was their first view of the snow-covered Alps. How majestic they were!

At one point the stewardess came to speak to them. "Some day you must come back and tour Switzerland," she said. "At the foot of these great mountains are wide green fields filled with beautiful wild flowers. And all the time you can hear the tinkling bells on the cattle and sheep that are grazing there."

"I suppose they need lots of cattle," said Jean, chuckling, "to make all that wonderful Swiss cheese."

"Yes." The stewardess smiled. "Switzerland certainly exports plenty of it and milk chocolate too."

Jean turned to Louise, who sat beside her. "I hope we have time to visit Switzerland later. I'd love to send Chris and Ken a gigantic cheese in return for the fruit."

When the plane landed in Frankfurt, the Danas and their friends were intrigued with the modern airport. They found themselves caught up in the large stream of people walking to the passport control booths. From there they advanced to the baggage claim area to wait for their suitcases.

"After we go through customs," said Aunt Harriet, "I think we'll try to get accommodations outside the city. I was reading in a travel booklet on the plane about this delightful spot. And it's on the way to the old castle."

Near the customs counter in the big airport building stood a dark, heavy-set man of about fifty. When he heard the official mention the Danas' name, the stranger stepped up to them.

Smiling, he said, "Captain Dana has been in touch with me and asked me to act as interpreter and guide while you're here. My name is Fritz Webelmann." He showed them a cablegram from Uncle Ned.

"That is very kind," said Aunt Harriet. "You speak flawless English. You're not a German?"

The man laughed. He said that he was an American of German parentage.

"I am spending the summer in Germany doing some research," he said. "But I have a lot of time on my hands and will be happy to give you as much of it as you may need."

Fritz Webelmann said he had rented an old American limousine and would take the group wherever they wanted to go. Aunt Harriet gave him the name of the inn.

"It's a very nice place," he said. "As soon as you've claimed your luggage, we'll start."

The bags were stowed inside. Louise and Jean climbed into the front of the high, old car. The other passengers seated themselves in the rear, back of the baggage.

"I feel like a sardine in an undersized can," Doris remarked as the car left the airport.

Soon the road which Webelmann took went up a steep hill. Halfway to the top, the passengers began to feel uneasy about his driving. The man was riding precariously near the edge of the road where it dropped off into a ravine! As Aunt Harriet was about to ask that he move the car to a safer position, the engine died.

"Oh, this old bus!" Webelmann cried out in disgust. He opened the door on his side, got out, and started for the front of the car.

At that moment the limousine began to roll backward. Doris shrieked and Evelyn held her breath.

Louise quickly reached over and yanked on the emergency brake. It failed to hold the car. The next instant the old limousine went down the embankment and turned over!

CHAPTER XVII

Trespassing Forbidden!

THERE was complete silence for a few seconds after the accident, then groans and screams. The old car, blocked by a heavy clump of bushes, had swerved and turned on its side some feet down the embankment. Inside, passengers and baggage lay in a jumbled mass.

"Oh, my back!" Aunt Harriet moaned. Then she added, "Louise! Jean! Doris! Evelyn! Are you —are you all right?"

One by one the girls responded and began to untangle themselves from the wreckage. Louise and Jean climbed out first, gently lifting Aunt Harriet, who could not straighten up.

"I'm afraid my back is sprained," the woman said, wincing with pain. "Are you girls *sure* you're all right?"

All were bruised and scratched but seemed to have suffered no major injuries. Suddenly they wondered where Fritz Webelmann was. Looking up the embankment, they saw him inching his way down.

"Thank goodness you're all alive!" he said. "That old piece of junk never should have been rented to me. I think you folks ought to sue the company."

"Never mind that now," said Louise. "The question is, what are we going to do? My aunt's back has been injured and we'll need other transportation right away."

Webelmann offered to go for help, saying he would return shortly. He scrambled up the hillside and disappeared. Five minutes went by, then ten.

"Mr. Webelmann is taking a terribly long time," Jean complained. Her head was aching badly and she noticed that the other girls were ghostly pale. "I'll go up to the road. If anyone comes along, I'm going to stop him and ask for help. We must get Aunt Harriet to a doctor."

She and Evelyn went up the incline and stood at the edge of the road. Another ten minutes went by. "Doesn't anyone ever go along the back roads here?" Jean fumed.

The words were hardly out of her mouth when the girls heard the purr of a motor. A couple of seconds later a car approached from around a bend beyond them. They waved for it to stop.

"Do you speak English?" Jean asked the driver, a middle-aged man.

"Yes," he replied. "Can I be of help?"

Jean told him about the accident and the fact that the man who was supposed to bring help had not yet returned. The driver alighted and looked down the embankment.

"*Ach!*" he exclaimed. "I am a *Doktor*. I will help you."

"A doctor!" Jean exclaimed thankfully. "How fortunate!"

As the physician inched his way down the slope, he said he was Dr. Mueller, from Frankfurt. The girls introduced themselves.

After examining Aunt Harriet, Dr. Mueller said that her back was badly sprained and she would have to rest in bed for a few days. He then asked where the Americans were staying. When they told him and said they were on their way there from the airport, he raised his eyebrows.

"You are going in the opposite direction," he said. "You must have taken the wrong turn."

At this announcement the Danas and their friends looked knowingly at one another. Apparently Fritz Webelmann had brought them here on purpose. It looked as though he had planned to let the car roll down the hillside, hoping its passengers would be injured—perhaps even killed!

The same thought ran through all the Danas'

minds: Probably Webelmann had never been contacted by Captain Dana. The cablegram was a
fake! Instead, their "guide" was actually in league
with people who were trying to keep the Danas
from finding Carlo and the winking ruby! But
the sisters did not have proof enough to warrant
contacting the police.

"I will drive you to my office," Dr. Mueller
offered, "and examine all of you. Then you can
take a taxi to your hotel."

"Thank you very much," said Aunt Harriet.
"I will feel much better when I'm in bed."

Dr. Mueller and Jean carried Miss Dana up the
hillside and made her as comfortable as possible
in the physician's car. The other girls brought
the baggage and climbed in.

When they arrived at his office, he treated Aunt
Harriet first, then the girls.

"You are lucky," he said. "No internal injuries.
Just the sprained back. I will call a taxi for you."

It was nearly an hour's drive to the inn where
they planned to stay. The quaint wooden building was of Gothic architecture with long, narrow
casement windows. The travelers were assigned
to two very large rooms. Each contained two
double four-poster beds, with spotlessly clean,
starched muslin canopies.

Doris exclaimed in delight, then giggled. "Each
of these beds is large enough for four people to
sleep in!"

Jean turned down the coverlet of one and took out Aunt Harriet's nightgown, while Louise helped her undress. Beneath the cool sheets at last, the woman sighed in relief.

"My, it feels good to be here!"

Miss Dana slept only fitfully that night, but her nieces were not aware of it. They did not hear a sound until they awoke in the morning. After eating breakfast in their room, Louise and Jean asked Aunt Harriet if it would be all right to leave her alone. They were eager to start their sleuthing immediately.

"Go ahead," Aunt Harriet urged. "I feel much better. But watch out for Fritz Webelmann. If he really meant to harm us, he may try a second time."

"I'd like to rent a car," said Louise. "Then we can go into Frankfurt and also out to the castle whenever we wish."

Miss Dana gave her consent and Louise hurried downstairs to speak to the clerk at the desk about getting a car.

"Do you have an international driver's license?" the young man queried.

"Yes, I have," Louise replied, glad that she had had the foresight to obtain one in the United States before leaving.

The clerk telephoned to Frankfurt and an hour later the small, rented automobile stood at the door. The driver said it would be necessary for

Louise to go back to the city to sign certain papers before taking the car. The four girls climbed in and rode to Frankfurt to attend to this formality.

After that was done, Jean said to her friends, "Let's stop at a police station and ask if they have any record of Carlo Marzi or Fritz Webelmann being wanted by the police."

Upon reaching the *Polizeiamt*, Louise and Jean went inside. The officer at the desk was a stern-looking man with a big black mustache. But he smiled pleasantly at the girls and greeted them in English. When he heard their request, he looked through his files for any reference to the two men.

"I do not have either of their names here," the *Wachtmeister* said.

"Carlo Marzi is an expert at making artificial gems," Louise told the officer. "Would the police, by any chance, be looking for a man who fits Carlo's description? Maybe he's using an assumed name."

Again the sergeant consulted his file. Finally he shook his head. Louise and Jean were overjoyed. So far as the police were concerned, Carlo was an innocent man!

When the *Wachtmeister* inquired why the girls wanted to locate Carlo, they told him about his brother Gino's request.

"We're also here on another errand," said Louise. "We girls are going up now to the old Kronen castle to look around."

the entire valley below. Some distance beneath it they came upon a large sign which had been planted directly in the middle of the road. It read:

BETRETEN VERBOTEN! GEFAHR!

"Well, we can't drive any farther," said Louise, as she got out and the others followed. "But we don't have to pay any attention to the sign not to trespass. We have Frau Marzi's permission to look around here."

"Even if there's danger," Jean added, "as the warning says."

The girls picked up the tools and started forward. But they had not gone twenty feet when a man wearing a guard's uniform appeared from around a bend.

Fritz Webelmann!

Pretending not to recognize the girls, the American held up his hand and said, "Halt! Visitors are not allowed here!"

"But, Mr. Webelmann—" Louise began.

"Get out! Hurry, or you'll be sorry!"

CHAPTER XVIII

Dungeon Prisoners

FRIGHTENED by the unfriendly expression on Webelmann's face, Evelyn and Doris backed away. Louise and Jean, however, stood their ground.

"We have permission from the owner to come here and we're not leaving!" Louise stated flatly.

An ugly expression came over Webelmann's face. "Things have altered since you got that permission. In fact, this property has changed hands. I'm in charge here now and you're going to do what I say."

Jean turned red with anger. Pointing a finger at Fritz Webelmann, she cried out, "I don't believe you're the guard at this place at all. You're an impostor! What's more, you never had a cablegram from our Uncle Ned. You just wanted to get rid of us and you almost succeeded. Why, you might have killed us, letting the car go over that embankment!"

The man's eyes blazed. Striding forward, he grabbed the shovel from Jean's hands and waved it at them menacingly.

"Get out of here!" he shouted. "Get out if you value your lives!"

Before the girls could reply, they were astounded by the sudden appearance of a policeman.

"Put down that shovel!" he ordered Webelmann in English. He walked directly toward the man and took the tool away. "What's the meaning of this?"

Webelmann did not answer. Instead, he asked, "Where did you come from?"

"The Frankfurt police sent word for a *Schutzmann* to hurry up here," the officer replied. "They knew these girls were on their way here and thought they might need some help. They were right!"

Louise and Jean exchanged swift glances. That blessed *Wachtmeister!*

As Webelmann remained silent, Louise told the *Schutzmann* the complete story of their acquaintance with the guard. The policeman scowled when he heard the part about the automobile accident.

"We'll check everything," he said. "But this I do know: The castle has no guard. Will you young ladies come along and prefer charges against this man, please?"

Louise and Jean were eager to start investigating the castle, and asked the officer if it would be all right for Doris and Evelyn to accompany him. The policeman nodded.

"Before you go, officer," said Louise, "would you mind doing me a favor and search Webelmann's pockets? It's just possible that he has stolen something from the castle."

"That's a good idea," the officer agreed.

To the girls' relief, there was no ruby in Webelmann's pockets—nothing except a small amount of money and two large old-fashioned keys.

"Perhaps those keys unlock some secret rooms in the castle," said Jean excitedly. "May we try them?"

As the officer handed over the keys, Webelmann suddenly became ferocious. He picked up a shovel and tried to strike the policeman on the head. As the officer dodged, Webelmann grabbed the keys from Jean and started running toward the castle.

"Halt!" the policeman ordered.

Webelmann did not stop. But his dash for freedom was short-lived. The whole group went after him, and within a few moments he was caught, subdued, and handcuffed. The prisoner, snarling like a tiger, was led away. Evelyn and Doris followed.

"There *must* be something in the castle that Webelmann didn't want us to find," said Louise, as she and Jean trudged toward the ancient building.

The older girl carried a shovel, her sister a pick. Presently the girls stopped to gaze at the ruined edifice. It was extensive and parts of every section were still standing. Two of the corners were topped with circular towers.

In the center part of the hollow, square building the girls could see what was left of a broad second-floor gallery. A third area, at right angles to the middle section, contained a large, semicircular opening resembling the entrance to a tunnel.

"We must be standing in what was once the courtyard," Louise remarked.

"Yes," her sister agreed, "and how magnificent the whole thing must have been!"

Louise whispered in Jean's ear, "Do you suppose Carlo could be imprisoned here somewhere? And if so, perhaps one of the keys in my pocket will open the door to his cell?"

Jean nodded, saying, "It would explain Webelmann's frantic efforts to get back the keys."

"I wonder where the most likely place would be," Louise said slowly.

Jean suddenly recalled Professor Jensen's story about the dungeons in one of the old German castles. She mentioned this to Louise and said:

"Let's hunt for a dungeon. Come on!"

Jean headed for the tunnellike entrance. Louise was close on her sister's heels as they started along the stone passageway. The place was dank and musty and the farther in they went, the darker it became. Just as the tunnel was becoming too dark for them to see where they were going, Jean exclaimed excitedly:

"Here's a door, Louise! Maybe this is a dungeon!"

Quickly she produced the two keys from her pocket. The first one did not fit the lock and for a moment the sisters became discouraged. But their hopes rose again when the second key turned. The heavy iron door swung inward.

"It *is* a dungeon!" Louise whispered in awe.

High in the far wall was a small opening with iron bars across it. The window let in enough light for the girls to make out the contents of the room. Along one wall stood a long bench on which could be seen small, shining objects.

Just inside the door Louise stumbled into a lantern. Hooked onto its handle was a box of paper matches. Quickly she lighted the lantern and the girls peered at the bench.

"A jeweler's workroom!" Jean burst out, as she now saw that the glinting objects were gems of many colors.

"Do you think these are real?" Jean asked her sister in awe.

Louise shrugged. "If they're imitations, they're certainly good ones." She had read an interesting article in the *Balaska's* library on the use of ruby dust. When fused in an electric furnace, gems

"Do you think these gems are real?"
Jean asked.

were created that looked, except to an expert, like those fashioned by nature.

"Isn't this an electric furnace?" Louise said, pointing to a small stove with batteries attached.

This, together with the various types of tools and burners on the bench, led the girls to believe that artificial gems were being made here.

"Do you suppose," said Louise, "that this could be Carlo's hide-out?"

"It's a good guess," Jean replied. "But since he's not here, we must be wrong about his being a prisoner."

Before Jean had a chance to answer, the door to the dungeon suddenly swung shut. Both girls rushed forward to open it. But though they lifted the latch and pulled the door, it would not open.

"Jean," said Louise, as a horrifying thought struck her, "maybe we've been locked in!"

Both girls began pounding on the door with all their might. As the sounds died away, their suspicions were confirmed. From the corridor came a sardonic, self-satisfied laugh!

"Let us out of here!" Jean demanded.

There was no reply and the imprisoned girls could hear footsteps receding up the passageway. In dismay Jean and Louise sagged against the door.

Finally Louise found her voice. "How could we have been so careless?" she asked. "Of course Fritz Webelmann had an accomplice!"

"Do you suppose it was Carlo?" Jean asked.

"Perhaps," her sister answered. "Well, there's only one hope for rescue—Evelyn and Doris."

Jean frowned. "I'm afraid that they'll be captured before they find us."

For several minutes neither girl spoke. Then thoughts of escape began to take form.

"First of all," Louise whispered, "let's guard the door. If anyone opens it, we'll rush him and make our escape."

"All right."

The Danas' eyes roved the room for another possible exit. There was none, but high in one side wall they saw a grated opening similar to that of the window.

"I'd like to know what's on the other side," said Jean. "Let me stand on your shoulders, Louise, so I can take a look."

Quickly Louise squatted down and then hoisted her sister up. Jean gazed through the opening and saw that it was a dungeon similar to the one in which she and Louise were imprisoned.

Suddenly she clapped a hand to her mouth and gasped, "Oh, my goodness!"

CHAPTER XIX

A Grinning Stone Face

"WHAT do you see?" Louise called up to Jean.

"A man's asleep in the next dungeon!" Jean replied. "He looks like Angela. He may be Carlo!"

Softly she began calling his name. There was no response. She tried again, this time a little louder. The man turned but did not reply.

"He's not just sleeping," said Jean. "He looks as if he might be drugged!"

"If so," Louise concluded, "he *is* a prisoner! And that may mean he's innocent."

The girls had been so intent on Jean's discovery that they had completely forgotten about guarding the door. Now they heard the sound of a key turning in the lock. Instantly Jean jumped down from Louise's shoulders and the two girls took their positions at the door to rush whoever might open it.

The door swung wide and to their amazement

Doris, then Evelyn, walked in. "Oh, here you are!" Doris began. "We thought—"

The girl never finished the sentence. Quick as panthers Louise and Jean had jumped a man who stood back of Evelyn in the corridor, before he had a chance to close the door. Taken off guard, he was easily subdued and dragged inside. For safety's sake, Louise removed the key from the lock and put it in her pocket. Jean guarded the door.

The man glared at his captors and began talking fast and angrily in German. The girls could understand only a little of what he was saying, but they gathered that he was pleading to be set free. He said he was innocent of any wrongdoing.

"What's it all about?" asked Evelyn, who had been looking on in amazement. "This man met us outside and said he was a tourist—at least, that's what we assumed from his German."

Doris added, "We asked him if he had seen two girls and he nodded yes. He crooked his finger for us to follow him, as if he were going to show us where you were."

Louise told the Danas' side of the story. Doris gasped. "Do you mean this man was going to make us prisoners, too?"

"I'm afraid so," Louise replied. "But we're going to turn the tables on him."

Pushing the man against the far wall of the dungeon, the girls quickly backed out the door and locked it. He protested volubly and kicked the locked door, but the girls paid no attention.

Louise was already taking the second key out of her pocket. "Oh, I hope this unlocks the other dungeon!" she said softly.

The other girls waited anxiously as she put the key into the door. "It works!" she cried out excitedly.

The door creaked eerily on its hinges. Louise asked Evelyn and Doris to stand guard in the corridor, and the Danas entered the room.

The commotion had failed to awaken the sleeping man. Even a gentle shaking by Jean brought no response.

"Let's carry him out into the fresh air," Louise suggested. "Maybe he'll revive and tell us his story."

As soon as they had him out in the sunlight and lying on some soft matted vines, the sisters slapped the young man's cheeks gently. In a little while he opened his eyes and looked at them dazedly. He began to murmur in Italian, *"Mama, Mama, sono in Paradiso? Sono morto?"*

Louise smiled at him sympathetically. "You are alive," she replied, "and not in heaven. Aren't you Carlo Marzi?"

The question startled the young man into reality. "Yes, I am Carlo Marzi. But why did my jailers let me out? And who are you?"

As briefly as possible Louise told the story from the beginning. Carlo cried out in anger when he heard about Gino's condition, brought on by the false story of Carlo's embezzlement and disappearance. Carlo shook his fist and declared he would track down the gang who was guilty of adding insult to the torture he had borne.

"Please try to be calm," Louise begged him. "Just think how much of the mystery has been solved already. When your brother learns that you have been found and are innocent, I'm sure his memory will be restored."

Jean asked who had imprisoned Carlo and why. He said that it was Fritz Webelmann.

"He learned through friends that I was coming to the Kronen castle to hunt for the winking ruby. After I spent days searching here, without finding it, Webelmann and another man captured me. After that, I was forced to make artificial gems and imitate beautiful rings from sketches given me."

"We had a little trouble with Webelmann ourselves," Jean spoke up. "You'll be glad to know that he's now in jail."

"*Ammerivole!*" Carlo cried out, smiling for the first time.

"And his helper is a prisoner in the dungeon next door to yours," said Evelyn.

"I owe a great deal to you girls," said Carlo,

looking at them gratefully. "I've been a prisoner for over two years. Everything was taken away from me, even the keys to my home."

"We guessed as much," said Jean, and she told about the visit of the Dottis and Sal Riccio to the house. Carlo said he had never heard of these people.

"They must be the ones who were receiving the jewelry I made."

"Didn't you ever try to run away?" Doris asked him.

Carlo shook his head sadly. "Webelmann told me that if I ever tried to, my family would be killed."

"The beast!" Jean cried out.

Carlo said he surmised that Webelmann had known there was a possibility of the girls' looking around the castle. To avoid their seeing or hearing his prisoner, the cruel man had put some sleeping drug in Carlo's food.

"But I must not talk any more about unfortunate things," the jewelry craftsman said. "I am too happy now."

The Danas, although glad that they had found Carlo alive—and not responsible for any wrongdoing—were disappointed to learn that he had not found the winking ruby. They asked him if he had searched the castle and the grounds.

"I searched about everywhere," the young man replied. "When I first came to Germany, I did a lot of research and learned that a valuable gem had once been embedded in the eye of a gargoyle. I thought this might mean the winking ruby. But in all this heap of ruins I did not find one gargoyle."

Louise and Jean, who had been kneeling as they talked to the reclining Carlo, now jumped excitedly to their feet. There was still a chance of finding the winking ruby!

"Did you do much digging?" Jean asked Carlo. "I mean, around the castle walls."

"No," Carlo answered.

Louise was already darting here and there, trying to reconstruct in her mind what the old castle must have looked like before the siege. Jean joined her and they gazed first at one pile of rubble, then another. Finally Jean said:

"I believe there might have been some decoration above the gallery. Maybe there was a gargoyle, or something like one, among them. Anyway, let's dig here, Louise."

The place was overgrown with bushes and the Danas asked the assistance of the others to pull out the shrubs. When this was done, Jean further loosened the dirt with the pick, while Louise used the shovel.

"There's something hard down here," Louise said a moment later. She brushed off a square foot of dirt to reveal part of a stone slab beneath.

Feverishly Jean and Louise cleared a larger

area. Part of a face, carved in the slab, began to show. By this time Doris and Evelyn were down on hands and knees with Carlo, clawing at the dirt until the figure's whole head was revealed.

"The winking ruby!" Doris shrieked.

For a moment everyone stared in awe at the face—a grinning Teutonic god with curly hair and beard. *Embedded in one of his eyes was a glinting ruby!* The other eye was closed.

Then Doris began to dance around exuberantly. "The mystery is solved! Everything is wonderful! Now Angela and Tony can get married!"

"Yes," said Carlo joyously, and the others grinned in delight. "And my family's rightful heritage restored!"

From his pocket the young Italian produced a small pointed tool and began to chisel around the edges of the gem. Presently he looked up and said:

"I could work faster with the proper tools. Would you girls mind going back to the dungeon where you found me and getting a small tool chest that's under the cot?"

The Danas volunteered to go. But before leaving, Louise said, "Just to be sure no one will discover our secret, I suggest that Evelyn and Doris act as guards. How about going a little way down the road, girls, to hold off any curious people. If somebody shows up, just whistle and Carlo can cover up this ruby."

The others thought this a wise idea. Evelyn and

Doris ran off, while Louise and Jean hurried back to the dungeon. As they unlocked the door to Carlo's former cell, a sense of foreboding came over the girls. The spooky atmosphere of the prison and the thought of the captive in the next room made the Danas' pulses quicken.

"But I'm silly," Louise told herself. "I ought to be dancing with joy."

Jean grabbed Carlo's tool chest and Louise hurriedly locked the door behind them. The sisters hastened up the corridor and rushed back to the spot where the treasure had been unearthed. To their consternation, Carlo was sprawled on the ground unconscious.

The winking ruby was gone!

CHAPTER XX

The Winking Ruby

THE DANA girls looked at each other in dismay. They had found the missing Carlo and located the fabulous ruby, only to have it snatched from them!

"We shouldn't have left Carlo alone," Louise murmured as she bent over to give him first aid.

"At least they didn't make him a prisoner," said Jean. "He's still a free man and can go back to his family." But both girls knew that the Marzis would be extremely disappointed to learn that the valuable ruby had been found, then lost again.

"Maybe the thief can be caught," said Louise, taking heart. "Jean, we ought to notify the police right away about this. Get the car keys out of my purse and ask Evelyn and Doris to go to the nearest station."

"You're right," said Jean. "That thief can't be very far away."

She hurried off. In less than two minutes Jean was telling the story to Evelyn and Doris, who were still keeping watch at the road.

"How dreadful!" Evelyn exclaimed. "We didn't see anyone go down the road. But we'll get the police, anyway."

The two girls ran to the rented car, and Evelyn took the wheel. She backed around, then started down the steep hillside as fast as she dared.

Doris's eyes scanned the area around, hoping to catch a glimpse of the thief. As the car rounded the last sharp turn, she cried out excitedly:

"Evelyn! There go a man and a woman!"

The couple had emerged from the woods on the mountainside to the girls' right and were running toward a car parked on the highway. When they heard Evelyn's automobile, the man and woman glanced back.

"They're Enrico and Lena Dotti!" Doris cried out. "We must catch them!"

Evelyn put on speed to overtake the couple. But the castle road turned left and did not join the highway for over a hundred feet. By the time Evelyn reached the main road and took up the chase, the hypnotists were far in the distance.

"Oh, we'll never catch them!" Doris wailed.

"We'll do our best," said Evelyn determinedly.

The car sped along and for a while it looked as if they might overtake the thieves. But suddenly the road ahead made a sharp turn. The Dottis' car zoomed out of sight and by the time Evelyn reached the same spot, the girls could see no sign of the fugitives' automobile. A minute later they came to a three-forked crossroad.

"Which road shall we take?"

Doris felt they should give up the chase. "We might take the wrong road and waste more time. I vote we stop at the next house and telephone the police."

But this was not necessary. Just as they were starting up again, a police car came from the center crossroad. Evelyn hailed it. To her delight, the officer at the wheel proved to be the same one who had taken Webelmann into custody.

"How are you making out?" he called across, smiling. "Any more prisoners for me?"

His smile changed to disbelief as Doris revealed what had happened. He said he had not passed any couple in a car.

"Please have the police go after them," Evelyn begged. She described the Dottis and the car they were driving.

"I certainly will," the officer said. Picking up the police-car microphone, he spoke in German for several seconds. When he clicked off the radio, he told the girls several men would be sent out immediately to cover all roads.

"You'd better go back to your friends," he advised.

"Can you come with us?" Evelyn asked him.

"We forgot to tell you that we have a prisoner in the castle."

Evelyn told him about the man who had imprisoned the Danas and how they in turn had captured him.

"Very good," the policeman said. "I'll make another call and then go with you." He notified headquarters of his change in plans, then followed the girls in his car.

When the trio arrived at the castle, Carlo was just regaining consciousness. As the young man's mind cleared, he gazed down at the grinning Teutonic god carved into the stone slab.

"The ruby," he said, feeling in his pocket. "Where is it?" he asked in alarm.

Reluctantly Louise explained what she thought had happened, trying to soften the news. Carlo said he had seen no one but had felt the knockout blow.

"The thieves will be captured," Evelyn said hopefully. She told about seeing the Dottis flee and of the police cordon.

"I only hope," said Doris, "that Enrico and Lena don't hide the winking ruby before they're caught, or manage to pass it along to someone else."

This possibility had not occurred to the others and they became worried. The policeman said he would find out what he could. From his pocket he pulled a small two-way radio and contacted headquarters.

Carlo now turned to the girls and whispered, "While I was alone here, I managed to chisel the ruby out of the eye. Then I made a discovery. *It is not the winking ruby!*"

"What!" Jean cried out softly. "How did you know?"

Carlo said that the one they had found was a red garnet with a single refraction.

"A ruby," he went on, "shows a good double refraction—that is, a natural ruby does. And it is always hexagonal in shape. That is a way of telling a real ruby from one that is manufactured."

"Then there's still a chance of finding the winking ruby!" Jean cried excitedly.

Carlo shook his head. "No, I am afraid the real one is gone forever."

The policeman stopped speaking on his radio and turned to the girls, a smile on his face. "I have good news for you—very good news. Mr. and Mrs. Dotti have been arrested. They had the ruby, which the police took from them. Also, the Dottis' accomplice, Sal Riccio, has been apprehended by the Italian police. Through him a great deal of loot has been recovered from an Italian jeweler who was in league with the gang.

"Among the articles were several rings, including a ruby, belonging to a Mrs. Cracken and a ruby ring owned by a Miss Rosamunde la Mer. Dotti confessed that he had substituted her ring for a fake one, which he had cleverly caused her to drop overboard to cover his guilt."

Evelyn smiled broadly. "That means Mrs. Cracken will have to eat her accusation against you Danas!"

"Your American police have done their work, too," the officer said. "A red-haired man who delivered a snake to the Danas' stateroom is in jail in New York City! He is one of the jewel thieves and sent a threatening letter to Gino Marzi."

Doris exclaimed. "The whole mystery is solved, and when Gino hears this, surely his memory will be restored!"

"Well," said the policeman, "I certainly am glad I had some small part in this case. And as you Americans say, my hat is off to you Dana girls!"

He saluted the sisters, then added, "Where will I find your prisoner?"

Louise gave the officer the keys to both dungeons and pointed to the tunnellike entrance. He strode off.

Doris sat down on the ground near Carlo. Taking his hand in hers, she said, "I'm so sorry that you didn't find the real winking ruby."

Suddenly an idea came to Louise. "Carlo," she said excitedly, "remember what your ancestor, the Baroness Kathryn von Kronen said? Why would she call her gem the winking ruby and then put it in plain sight in the open eye?"

Jean grabbed her sister's arm enthusiastically. "You mean the real ruby might be under the eye which is closed?"

"Yes."

"You may be right," Carlo said, his eyes brightening with hope.

Opening his tool kit, which still lay beside him, the craftsman began chipping away at the stone which formed the eyelid of the winking Teutonic god. The others watched breathlessly. Presently something deep red beneath glinted in the sunlight!

Hardly daring to hope that Louise had guessed correctly, Carlo continued to chip away the stone. At last his efforts were rewarded.

"It is here!" he cried out. "The story is true!"

Embedded in the eye was an exquisite ruby. It glowed with a blood-red color.

Carlo, overcome with emotion, blinked up at the girls through tears. "This is the winking ruby! Nothing I can ever say or do could repay you for the wonderful work you have accomplished. We have the family heirloom. And what is even more important, my family can live together again without fear!"

"And Angela and Tony can get married," Doris said, sighing. "We must telegraph them as soon as we get to Frankfurt."

A period of silence followed. Louise gazed over the peaceful hillside, then at the ruined castle.

"May I know what your errand is?" the officer asked, a twinkle in his eye.

Jean grinned. "Did you ever hear of the winking ruby?"

The officer looked puzzled, then replied, "No, I'm sure that case is not in our records either."

The Danas told him the story of Baroness von Kronen's ruby, and Louise added, "We want to see what's left of the place where this interesting person lived."

"Have a good time," said the officer, and turned to answer his ringing telephone.

As the Danas left the *Polizeiamt*, Jean called Louise's attention to a hardware store across the street. She suggested that they buy two shovels and two picks, so that they could do some digging as well as other investigating at the castle.

"Good idea," said Louise.

The sisters did this errand, then joined their friends in the car and started for the castle. On the way out of the city they admired the attractive, tree-shaded streets, the fine stone mansions, and the beautiful parks.

When they reached the outlying territory, the girls began to feel that they were certainly wearing the wrong weight clothing. The sun was shining brightly and the temperature had risen. Everyone in cars or walking along the road was in summer attire. The Danas reflected on what they were wearing and giggled.

"I guess we're not properly dressed," said Jean, who had on a navy skirt and red sweater over a white blouse.

"And I'm beginning to feel kind of warm," added Louise, who that morning had put on a light-brown wool skirt, a yellow pull-over, and a white cardigan.

For several miles they rode along the Rhine River, intrigued by the many castles set on the peaks of the rugged hillsides. Presently they came to the site of the legend of the Lorelei.

"I guess those rocks could tell many a story," said Doris, sighing. "Think of all the sailors who lost their lives there when they looked up on the hillside to see the beautiful siren singing, and wrecked their boats."

Jean smiled. "And Lorelei wasn't even there!"

"Or so some people say," Doris defended herself. "Who knows after all these years whether or not she was there luring those poor men to their deaths?"

An hour later Louise turned off the main road. She drove the car up a winding, narrow, dirt lane. Ahead of them the girls could see part of one tower of the old castle.

"Isn't this romantic?" Doris burst out, her eyes gleaming in excitement.

"It sure is," Jean agreed, as they wound up the steep road.

The castle stood on a promontory overlooking

Would another mystery as fascinating come their way? It did, when they solved *The Ghost in the Gallery*.

Meanwhile, Jean had reached into her purse for a pencil and pad and now thoughtfully wrote a message. The corners of her mouth turned up as she finished.

"Sis, you look as if you'd swallowed the canary," Louise said. "What did you write?"

"A cablegram to Uncle Ned." Jean handed the note to Louise as Evelyn and Doris pressed close for a look.

All three chuckled as Louise read aloud:

> " '*Dear Uncle Ned,*
> *The girls found me and Carlo.*
> *Here's winking at you.*
> *Ruby*' "